OUT OF THE DARKNESS

The thing had decided to end the game of cat and mouse and was making a beeline for them. They must reach the trees or they were doomed.

Suddenly the hummock appeared, a low mound bisected by the trail. The trees were not many, but some had thick trunks and might resist being uprooted. Emmeline raced to one, hooked her hands under Halette's arms, and practically heaved her at the lowest limbs, shouting, "Grab hold and climb!"

"What about you?"

Emmeline whirled. The massive monster was almost on top of them. She jerked her rifle to her shoulder and took aim. But even as she fired, and her daughter screamed, Emmeline knew these were her last moments on earth. Her rifle boomed but it had no effect, and then the thing was on her. Emmeline tried to be brave—she tried not to scream—but God, the pain, the searing, awful ripping and rending.

It seemed to go on forever.

THE TRAILSMAN

#329

BAYOU TRACKDOWN

by

Jon Sharpe

A SIGNET BOOK

SIGNET
Published by New American Library, a division of
Penguin Group (USA) Inc., 375 Hudson Street,
New York, New York 10014, USA
Penguin Group (Canada), 90 Eglinton Avenue East, Suite 700, Toronto,
Ontario M4P 2Y3, Canada (a division of Pearson Penguin Canada Inc.)
Penguin Books Ltd., 80 Strand, London WC2R 0RL, England
Penguin Ireland, 25 St. Stephen's Green, Dublin 2,
Ireland (a division of Penguin Books Ltd.)
Penguin Group (Australia), 250 Camberwell Road, Camberwell, Victoria 3124,
Australia (a division of Pearson Australia Group Pty. Ltd.)
Penguin Books India Pvt. Ltd., 11 Community Centre, Panchsheel Park,
New Delhi - 110 017, India
Penguin Group (NZ), 67 Apollo Drive, Rosedale, North Shore 0632,
New Zealand (a division of Pearson New Zealand Ltd.)
Penguin Books (South Africa) (Pty.) Ltd., 24 Sturdee Avenue,
Rosebank, Johannesburg 2196, South Africa

Penguin Books Ltd., Registered Offices:
80 Strand, London WC2R 0RL, England

First published by Signet, an imprint of New American Library,
a division of Penguin Group (USA) Inc.

First Printing, March 2009
10 9 8 7 6 5 4 3 2 1

The first chapter of this book previously appeared in *Texas Triggers*, the three
hundred twenty-eighth volume in this series.

PUBLISHER'S NOTE
This is a work of fiction. Names, characters, places, and incidents either are
the product of the author's imagination or are used fictitiously, and any resem-
blance to actual persons, living or dead, business establishments, events, or
locales is entirely coincidental.

The publisher does not have any control over and does not assume any
responsibility for author or third-party Web sites or their content.

The Trailsman

Beginnings . . . they bend the tree and they mark the man. Skye Fargo was born when he was eighteen. Terror was his midwife, vengeance his first cry. Killing spawned Skye Fargo, ruthless, cold-blooded murder. Out of the acrid smoke of gunpowder still hanging in the air, he rose, cried out a promise never forgotten.

The Trailsman they began to call him all across the West: searcher, scout, hunter, the man who could see where others only looked, his skills for hire but not his soul, the man who lived each day to the fullest, yet trailed each tomorrow. Skye Fargo, the Trailsman, the seeker who could take the wildness of a land and the wanting of a woman and make them his own.

The Louisiana swamp, 1861—where death came in many guises and many sizes.

1

The night was moonless but the mother wasn't worried.

Emmeline had been born and bred in the Atchafalaya Swamp. She knew the bayous and cypress haunts as city women knew streets and alleys. She was at home here.

So it was that on a hot, muggy summer night, Emmeline and her youngest, Halette, started out from the settlement for their cabin. The trails were as familiar to her as garden paths to a Southern belle. Emmeline thought nothing of the fact that the swamp crawled with snakes and alligators. She had her rifle and she was a good shot.

But as they were leaving her best friend's shack, Simone took her aside. "Maybe you should stay the night, *oui*? Start back in the morning fresh and rested."

"*Non*," Emmeline said. "We can be home in a couple of hours if we don't stop to rest too often."

"Your daughter is only eight. You expect too much of her," Simone criticized.

"No more than I expected of myself at her age." Emmeline kissed Simone on the cheek. "Don't worry. We'll be fine. I've have done this countless times, have I not?"

"Even so," Simone said, and, glancing at Halette, she lowered her voice. "There have been stories."

"Oh, please."

"You've heard them. About the people who have gone missing. About a creature that is never seen but only heard. About the blood and the bones." Simone shuddered. "I tell you, they terrify me."

"Oh, please," Emmeline said again. "Am I a child to be made timid by horror tales?"

Emmeline and little Halette had been hiking under the stars for over an hour now. They were deep in the swamp, well past the last of the isolated cabins that dotted the watery domain of the cottonmouth, save one—their own cabin. And they still had a long way to go.

"I'm tired, *Mère*," Halette remarked. She had her mother's oval face and fair complexion and her beautiful auburn hair.

"There is a spot ahead. It's not far. I suppose we can rest there for a few minutes."

"*Merci.*"

The spot Emmeline was thinking of was a grassy hummock. The trail, after many twists and turns, often with water lapping at both sides, presently brought them there, and Halette, with a sigh of relief, sank down, curling her legs under her.

"Watch out for snakes," Emmeline cautioned.

"I'm too tired to care."

The breeze was strong. It brought with it the night sounds of the great swamp: the croak of frogs, the bellow of gators, the scream of a panther, and the shrieks of prey. These were sounds Emmeline was used to. She had heard them every night of her life. She gave them no more thought than a city woman would give the clatter of wagon wheels.

Emmeline sat down next to Halette, and her daughter leaned against her, saying quietly, "It's pretty out here."

"*Oui.* I have always loved the swamp. Many people are afraid of it, but to us who live in it, it is part of us. It is in our blood and in our breath, and we can never be afraid."

"I am now and then. When I am in our cabin alone at night and I hear noises."

Emmeline squeezed Halette's shoulder. "That's normal, little one. When I was young as you, I would get scared, too. I imagined all sorts of things that were not real. Eventually you outgrow such silliness."

"I will try not to be afraid, for you."

Mother and daughter shared smiles, and the mother hugged the daughter, and it was then, from out of the benighted fastness of water and cypress and reeds, that there came a sound that caused the mother to stiffen and the daughter to gasp. It was a low rumbling, neither roar nor grunt yet a little of both, which rose to a piercing squeal and then abruptly stopped.

"What was that?" Halette exclaimed.

"I don't know," Emmeline admitted. "A gator, maybe."

"I never heard a gator do that. No bear, either. Yet it had to be something big. Really big."

"Whatever it was, it was far away."

"Was it? *Père* says that sometimes our ears play tricks on us. That what we think is far is close, and what we think is close is far."

Emmeline grinned and ruffled Halette's hair. "You worry too much. That is your problem." She rose. "Come. We should keep going. I do not want to take all night getting home."

They walked on, the mother holding the girl's hand, and if the girl walked so close that their hips brushed, the mother didn't say anything. They had gone several hundred feet and were in a belt of rank vegetation with solid ground all around when the strange sound was repeated. They both stopped.

"It's closer," Halette said.

"But still a ways off." Emmeline walked faster and was comforted by the old Sharps in the crook of her elbow. It held only one shot but it was powerful enough to bring down anything in the swamp. And she could hit a knothole in a tree at thirty paces.

"Wouldn't it be nice to sing?" Halette asked. "I like it when we sing."

So they sang, a new ditty popular with children called "The Pig Song" by a man named Burnand.

"There was a fiddler and he wore a wig. Wiggy, wiggy, wiggy, wiggy, weedle, weedle, weedle. He saved up his money and he bought a pig. Tweedle, tweedle, tweedle, tweedle, tweedle, tweedle, tweedle."

They were about to begin the second stanza when a rumbling grunt from out of the thick undergrowth brought them to a stop. Halette's fingernails dug so deep into Emmeline's palm they almost drew blood.

"It's really close, *Mère*."

"Don't worry. I have my rifle." But Emmeline was worried herself. She thought it might be a black bear, and if so, it had to be a big one and the big ones were hard to kill. A single shot to the brain or the heart was not always enough. She walked faster.

Somewhere off in the darkness a twig snapped.

"I don't like this," Halette said.

"Be brave. I'm right here." But inside Emmeline, a swarm of butterflies was loose in her stomach. Or was it moths, since it was nighttime? She smiled at her humor, and then lost the smile when something crunched off in the trees.

"Did you hear that?"

"Stay calm. It might be a deer."

"No deer made that sound we heard," Halette insisted. "Whatever it is, it's following us."

"That's preposterous." But Emmeline had the same suspicion. She shifted her rifle so the muzzle was pointed at the side of the trails the thing was on.

"Should we climb a tree? *Père* says that's the best thing to do when a bear is after you."

"Only if it's a large bear," Emmeline amended. "Small bears can climb as well as we can."

The undergrowth rustled and crackled. They stopped, peered hard to try to spot the cause, and the crackling stopped. When they moved on, the crackling began again.

"What *is* it, *Mère*?" Halette asked in stark fear.

"Stay calm," Emmeline said again. But deep inside she was just as scared. Whatever the thing was, it wasn't afraid of them. It was indeed stalking them and it didn't care if they knew it. Her palms grew slick with sweat and her mouth became dry.

For minutes that seemed like hours the taut tableau continued. Mother and daughter were glued to each other. Now and then the creature in the undergrowth grunted or snorted and the mother felt her youngest quake.

"I wish *Père* was here," the girl said, not once but several times.

The mother thought of their cabin, so near and yet so far, and her husband, and she felt a burning sensation in the pit of her stomach that brought bitter bile to her mouth. She swallowed the bile back down.

Simone had been right to take the tales seriously, and Emmeline had been wrong. Those people who vanished—they hadn't become lost or fallen to the Mad Indian or run into Remy Cuvier's cutthroats. Not that Remy would ever harm her, or any other Cajun, for that matter. The thing in the woods was to blame. She knew that as surely as she knew anything.

Then the growth thinned and ahead lay a stretch of swamp where the trail was no wider than a broad man's shoulders. Water lapped the edges. Here and there hummocks of land choked with growth broke the surface.

Emmeline's heart leaped in fragile hope. The thing could not get at them now without her seeing it. She would be able to get off a shot, and must make the shot count. Emboldened, she said for her daughter's benefit, "Let that animal show itself now and I will put a hole in its head."

Halette laughed a short, nervous laugh.

They redoubled their speed. A city girl using that serpentine trail in the dark of night would inch along like a turtle, but Emmeline and Halette were bayou born and bred, and to them a trail three feet wide was as good as a road. They covered a hundred yards, and there was no sign of the creature. Two hundred yards, and the only sounds were those of the insects, frogs and gators, a familiar chorus that soothed their troubled hearts.

"I guess it was nothing," Halette broke their silence, and laughed again.

No sooner were the words out of her young mouth than a loud splash warned them that something large was in the water.

"A gator," Emmeline said.

"Sure," Halette agreed.

But then the thing that made the splash grunted, and icy cold fear rippled down their spines.

"It's still following us!" Halette gasped.

"Perhaps it is something harmless." But Emmeline didn't believe that. Her fright was heightened by the thought that whatever that thing was, it must know about guns. How else to explain why it moved away from them when they came to the open water, yet still shadowed them?

"If only our cabin wasn't so far."

"We'll make it," Emmeline said, and patted Halette on the head. "I won't ever let anything happen to you."

"Frogs eat bugs and snakes eat frogs and gators eat snakes and frogs and people, too," Halette said softly.

It was a family saying. It stemmed from when their oldest, Clovis, was younger than Halette, and they were trying to make him understand that while the bayous and swamps were places of great beauty, they were also places of great danger. To a five-year-old boy, the world was a friend. It took some doing for Emmeline and Namo to convince Clovis that he must be wary of the many creatures that could do him harm. To that end, Emmeline came up with a rhyme to remind him. Silly, but it helped, and Clovis came to see that while the world was his friend, some of the creatures he shared the world with weren't friendly.

"Listen!" Halette exclaimed.

The thing was grunting and snorting in a frenzy,

and the splashing had grown so loud, the very swamp seemed to be in upheaval.

"It's fighting something!"

Emmeline thought so, too. A gator, perhaps. Or one of the huge snakes, rare but spotted from time to time by the human denizens of the great swamp. Town and city dwellers scoffed at the notion, saying snakes never grew to thirty meters or more and were never as thick around as large trees. But the swamp dwellers saw with their own eyes, and knew the truth.

There were other tales, too. Of things only talked about behind locked doors in the flickering glow of candles. Of goblins and ghosts and three-toed skunk apes. But Emmeline never believed in any of that. Her Namo did. He was as superstitious as a person could be, but he was a good provider and a good husband, so she put up with his charms and bones and rabbit's feet.

The splashing and grunting ended in a high-pitched squeal that climbed to an ear-piercing shriek.

Halette said, "Something is dying."

Emmeline went rigid with shock. She almost told her daughter that no, that wasn't it. The squeal wasn't the death cry of the loser; it was the cry of triumph of the victor. At last she realized what it was, and fear filled every fiber of her being. "Run," she said.

And they ran.

A hundred feet more would bring them to a hummock, and trees. Those trees, Emmeline hoped, would prove their salvation. She held her daughter's hand firmly and the two of them fairly flew. She could go faster, but Halette was at her limit.

"*Mère!*"

Emmeline had heard. The splashing was coming toward them. The thing had decided to end the game of cat and mouse and was making a beeline for them. They must reach the trees or they were doomed.

Suddenly the hummock appeared, a low mound bisected by the trail. The trees were not many, but some had thick trunks and might resist being uprooted. Emmeline raced to one, hooked her hands under Halette's arms, and practically heaved her at the lowest limbs, shouting, "Grab hold and climb!"

"What about you?"

Emmeline whirled. The massive monster was almost on top of them. She jerked her rifle to her shoulder and took aim. But even as she fired, and her daughter screamed, Emmeline knew these were her last moments on earth. Her rifle boomed but it had no effect, and then the thing was on her. Emmeline tried to be brave—she tried not to scream—but God, the pain, the searing, awful ripping and rending.

It seemed to go on forever.

2

Skye Fargo was a long way from the mountains and prairies he loved to roam. A big man, broad at the shoulder and slim at the hips, he sat a saddle as if born to it. He wore buckskins and a hat that was white when he bought it but now was a dusty shade of brown, and a red bandana. On his hip was a Colt. In his boot in an ankle sheath nestled a twin-edged Arkansas toothpick.

Fargo was close to Arkansas now, or as close as he had been in many a month. He was in Louisiana, in the backwater bayou country, winding along what the locals called a road but anyone else would call a path. It was pockmarked with hoofprints and rutted by more than a few wagon wheels.

So far the directions in the letter had been easy to follow. But then, finding something the size of the Atchafalaya Swamp was easy for a man who had an unerring instinct for finding his way anywhere. The Trailsman, folks called him, not because he followed known trails but because he broke new ones.

Skye Fargo had been where no whites ever set foot. He had explored vast tracts of untamed country overrun with hostile men and savage beasts. That he was still breathing said a lot about his ability to handle himself.

The trail was leading Fargo ever deeper into the swamp. As he rode he studied the riot of plant growth. Many were plants seldom if ever seen west of the Mississippi. Take magnolia trees, which Louisiana had plenty of. Oak trees and cypress were also common, the latter especially so in the swamp, where Spanish moss hung from many a limb. Flowers grew in profusion— lilies, orchids, jasmine and azaleas.

Honeysuckle was abundant. Fargo liked the sweet taste. It reminded him of many idle hours spent as a boy plucking and sucking.

Where there was a rich variety of plant life, there was invariably a rich variety of animal life. Louisiana was rife with deer and bear. Wildcats thrived. Muskrats plied the waterways. Raccoons and opossums and polecats were all over. Then there were the cougars, the alligators, and the snakes.

Fargo could do without the snakes. It was bad enough having to deal with rattlers. But here there were also cottonmouths and copperheads and a few coral snakes, or so he had been told.

Birds were as numerous as everything else. Warblers, robins, wrens. Sparrows, finches, woodpeckers. It went without saying that ducks and geese found all the water to their liking. As did brown pelicans.

Fargo breathed deep of the muggy, dank air. It didn't suit him. Give him the rarified heights of the Rocky Mountains any day. There was practically no humidity that high up.

The Ovaro nickered.

Fargo had learned the hard way to trust the stallion's senses, and he suspected that around the next bend he would see what he came so far to find. He was right.

The settlement of Gros Ville did not deserve the name. It consisted of scarcely twenty buildings. Half were shacks that looked fit to fall down at the next strong wind. One of the exceptions was a long log building. A sign in French read, *MOUILLE LANGUE*.

Fargo's French was spotty. As he drew rein at the hitch rail he wondered out loud, "What the blazes does that mean?"

"It means," said a sultry voice from the shadows under the overhang, "Wet Tongue."

10

"I like the sound of that." Fargo grinned, and sniffed. "Unless I miss my guess, it's the town tavern."

"*Oui,* monsieur," confirmed the sultry voice. "Come in and wet yours, if you like."

"Show yourself, why don't you?"

Into the sunlight stepped a beauty. Thick, shimmering black hair cascaded in curls over her shoulders. Her twin melons nearly burst her tight blue dress at the seams. But it was the face that drew Fargo's gaze. She had eyes as blue as his, with delicate arched eyebrows and an aquiline nose. Her lips were perfection: ripe and red, like cherries.

"Well, now," Fargo said. "How about if you join me in that tongue wetting? I'll wet yours and you can wet mine."

The lovely vision had a soft, melodious laugh. "Are you always *très* bold, monsieur?"

"Only around pretty ladies," Fargo said as he dismounted. Arching his back, he pressed a hand to his spine. "I've been in the saddle so long, I've forgotten what it's like to stand."

Again she laughed. "We do not see many of your kind here. You are a—what do they call it?—frontiersman?" She grinned impishly "You fight the red Indians who lift hair, and you kill the big bears that eat people, yes?"

"I avoid the hair lifters when I can," Fargo told her. "And I usually run from the big bears if they're out to eat me."

She liked to laugh, this woman. "You are a most funny man. I think I like you. *Quel est votre nom?*"

"How was that again?"

"What is your name, monsieur?"

Fargo told her.

"*Enchanté.* My name is Liana." She held out her hand. "Perhaps you would be so kind as to grace my establishment."

Pointing at the sign, Fargo said in mild surprise, "This tavern is yours?"

"*Oui*. My husband, Oliver, built it five years ago." Liana's features clouded. "When he died, I took it over."

"He couldn't have been that old."

"He wasn't. He was but one year older than I. It wasn't old age that claimed him." Sadness came over her.

"What then?"

Liana offered a hesitant smile. "I'd rather not talk about it, if you don't mind. Come. You must be thirsty on a hot day like this. And my liquor is the best for a hundred miles."

"Not just your liquor," Fargo said by way of a compliment while openly admiring her hourglass shape.

"I can see I am going to have trouble with you."

"Not me," Fargo said, taking her arm in his. "I'm as friendly a gent as ever lived."

"Perhaps too friendly, *non*?" Liana teased. "And so handsome, yes? Many ladies must find you *joli*."

"Enough drinks and I'll laugh at anything."

Liana blinked, then burst into hearty mirth. "Oh, monsieur. You are playing with me, yes?"

"Not yet. But maybe I'll get lucky." Fargo held the door for her and then followed her in. The interior was dark and musty and smelled of liquor and beer and cigar and pipe smoke.

"*Êtes-vous marié?*"

"There you go again." Fargo saw three men at a corner table and another at the bar. All were dressed pretty much the same, with white shirts, made of cotton, without collars, and pants that came down only as far as the knee, either red or indigo. They all wore caps and had knives at their waist. Their expressions were not what Fargo would call friendly.

Liana was saying, "Sorry. I will speak only English. I asked if you are married?"

Now it was Fargo's turn to laugh.

"I take it that was no? That is good. That is very good. A man so handsome should not have a fence around him." Liana went around the end of the bar.

12

"Now what will it be?" She motioned at a long shelf lined with every kind of hard spirit. "As you can see, I am well stocked."

Fargo fixed his gaze on her bosom. "You sure are."

Liana colored from her chin to her hairline. Leaning on her elbows, she said throatily, "I like you more and more, *joli* one. Will you ride on soon or can I persuade you to stay a while, perhaps?"

"I'm meeting a man," Fargo revealed. "But I'm a day early so I'll be here at least one night."

"*Très bien.* That is good. That is very good. I close at eleven and will be free for a moonlight walk should you care for my company."

"What if there's no moon?"

Liana chuckled, and put her hand on his wrist. "I am so happy you have come along."

Fargo heard chairs scrape and glanced at the mirror behind the bar. The three men at the table had risen and were coming toward him. The man in the center, a black-haired cuss with a scar on his chin, put his hand on the hilt of his knife. "Friends of yours?"

Liana looked, and flushed again, but this time with anger. "What do you want, Doucet? I am talking to this man."

"I can see that, *ma chère*," said the one with the scar with an accent typical of the swamp dwellers.

"I am not your dear, now or ever. You and your friends go back to your *Boureé.* I will not have you bother a customer."

The man called Doucet stepped close to Fargo and fingered his knife. But he was staring at Liana. "Is that all he is, *ma chère*? You seem very friendly with him."

"If I am it is none of your concern."

"You can say that, after our time in the glade? Are you so cold, then, that it was nothing to you?"

"Go back to your card game."

"First I am escorting your new friend outside," Doucet said. "Pitre, Babin and I would like words with him."

Fargo had been ignored long enough. He gave them

13

no warning. Pivoting, he drove his right fist into the pit of Doucet's gut, doubling the Cajun over. Still moving, he whipped around and streaked out his Colt as the other two went to jump him. The click of the hammer froze them in place. "I wouldn't, were I you, gents."

Doucet was on his knees, wheezing, his hands pressed to his stomach. "Bastard!" he spat.

"You brought it on yourself, lunkhead." Fargo wagged his Colt at the other two. "Help him up and tote him to your table and don't bother me again or the next time I won't be so charitable." He kept the Colt leveled until they were in their chairs, then twirled it into his holster. "Nice friends you have."

Doucet glared pure hate.

"I have known them since I was a small girl. One night I was lonely, and I went for a walk with Doucet. Just the one time, but ever since, he thinks I am his." Liana sighed. "Men. Kiss them and they act as if they own you."

"Not me," Fargo said with a grin. "I kiss and kiss and don't care to own anyone." Or be owned, he thought to himself.

"I am sorry for their behavior. Normally they would not have done that. But everyone is—how do you say?—on edge."

"What has them so prickly?"

Liana went to answer but caught herself. "Wait. Wouldn't you care for your drink first?"

"That's what I like," Fargo quipped. "A female who knows what's important in life." He pointed at a bottle of whiskey. "The Monongahela will do me."

Procuring a glass, Liana filled it to the brim and slid it across. "The first one is on me."

"You're a daisy," Fargo said.

Liana put her elbows on the bar and her chin in her hands. "As for the other, there is not just one cause. There are several. Some people say the Atchafalaya Swamp is under a curse."

Fargo took a sip and savored the burning sensation

that spread down his throat to his belly. "I'm not much for witches and black cats."

"If only that was all there is to it. But there is loose in the swamp much evil these days. There is the Mad Indian. There are Remy and his killers. And then there is the thing no one will talk about for fear they will be next."

"Tell me more," Fargo coaxed. "Start with that Indian you mentioned."

"No one knows his name or even what tribe he is from. We call him the Mad Indian. He wanders the far reaches of the swamp, and whenever someone sees him, he laughs and screams threats. But then he always runs off."

"Sounds loco to me," Fargo agreed. "And this Remy?"

"Ah. He is not mad, that one. He has killed a few times. Only outsiders, you understand. He has surrounded himself with other outcasts, and they roam where they please, doing as they will."

"You know for a fact he's killed people?"

"I do."

"Then why hasn't the law done something?"

"What law, monsieur? We are Cajuns. We are left alone, and we like it that way."

"You're saying there's no marshal or sheriff?"

"Oh, there is a sheriff, but he is far away, and we would never go to him anyway. We deal with our own problems."

Fargo swallowed some whiskey. There was more to this situation than he had been told. "And what was that other thing you mentioned? About something no one will talk about?"

Liana glanced about the room. Bending toward him, she lowered her voice. "The people live in terror, monsieur. Men, women, children have all gone missing. It is said a creature stalks the swamps, a creature such as the swamp has never known."

"I'm not much for tall tales, either."

"This is no tale, handsome one. I swear by all that

15

is holy that it is true. I knew some of those who vanished. They went into the swamp and never came back."

"People get lost. There are snakes. There are gators. There's quicksand. There's Remy and that Mad Indian."

"True. All true. But this is something else. One person actually saw the creature, and lived."

"And what did they say it was?"

Liana hesitated. "You will think me crazy."

"Try me."

"A monster, monsieur. A living, breathing monster."

3

The tavern began to fill up shortly after the sun went down. Out of the swamp they came, hardy men who made their living trapping and hunting and fishing. Pride was in their step and wariness in their eyes when they saw Fargo at a table playing solitaire. Fargo was an outsider, and the Cajuns didn't cotton to strangers in their midst.

Along about seven Liana came over to refill his glass and Fargo asked if there was any chance of getting something to eat. Half an hour later she brought over a tray. Cajun fare. Gumbo with sassafras leaves to start, then several pieces of boudin, or pork sausage, along with a dish for which Cajuns were rightly famed: jambalaya.

Fargo ate with enthusiasm. He hadn't had anything all day and was ravenous. As he was chewing some rice and green onions, there was a commotion outside, and the next moment a man who had to be in his fifties came through the door and barreled toward the bar. "A drink! And quick." The other Cajuns gathered around and there was an excited babble of Cajun French and English. Fargo overheard bits and snatches but not enough to tell him what the fuss was about.

Liana came over. "Do you see that man? He has just come from deep in the swamp. He says someone else has gone missing."

"Who?" Fargo asked, hoping it wasn't the man who sent for him.

"A friend of his. They have a cabin. The friend went out to chop wood and never came back."

"When was this?"

"Four days ago. The man looked and looked but couldn't find a trace. He says he will not go back. He is going off to New Orleans to live until people stop disappearing." Liana sadly shook her head. "He is not the first to leave and I expect he will not be the last."

Shortly after nine Fargo drifted outside to stretch his legs and check on the Ovaro. It would still be a couple of hours before Liana was free. He strolled the length of the single street and back again, listening to the crickets and the frogs and the other sounds that issued from the swamp. Moths fluttered at a shack window, drawn by the light.

Fargo was almost to the tavern when he turned to watch a black cat cross the street. His back was to the darkness, a mistake, as it turned out, because out of the dark rushed three men who pounced before he could draw. Two grabbed his arms and held fast while the third smirked and wagged a long-bladed knife.

"Did you think I would forgive and forget?" Doucet asked.

Fargo sighed. "It doesn't have to be like this. Let me go and there won't be any hard feelings."

"You jest. You struck me, remember? I do not know about where you come from, but no one strikes a Cajun and just walks away."

Fargo glanced at the men holding him and made one last try. "I have no quarrel with you."

Doucet uttered a sharp bark. "Do you hear him, Pitre? Do you hear him, Babin? He comes among us and spits on our honor and then tries to talk his way out of it."

"I was sent for by one of you," Fargo revealed. "I have his letter in my saddlebags."

"What do we care if you were invited or not? You are an outsider and that is all that counts." Doucet raised the blade so the tip was inches from Fargo's cheek. "Scream if you want. I don't care if Liana hears and is angry with me. I have this to do."

"You're a jackass."

"Another insult. Even as I hold a knife to your face. You are not strong on brains, outsider."

The Cajun holding Fargo's right arm said, "Enough. Do what you will but don't toy with him."

"What's the matter, Babin? No stomach for it?"

"I believe that when you need to hurt a man, you get it over with. You don't talk him to death."

"I agree," Pitre chimed in.

"And you call yourselves my friends?" Doucet said in considerable disgust. "But very well. I'll cut him and be done with it."

"No, you won't," Fargo said, and swept his boots up from the ground and slammed them against Doucet's chest. Doucet bleated in surprise and stumbled back. Instantly, Fargo shifted, throwing all his weight into throwing Pitre off-balance. He succeeded. Pitre lost his hold and fell to one knee. Babin, caught flat-footed, recovered and tried to trip Fargo and bring him down but Fargo unleashed an uppercut that sent Babin tottering.

Doucet came at him with the knife.

Fargo sidestepped, clamped both hands on the Cajun's arm, and drove his knee into Doucet's elbow. There was a *crack*, and Doucet stiffened and screeched. Fargo silenced him with a right cross that felled Doucet in his tracks.

Pitre and Babin sprang from opposite sides— Pitre with his arms out and his fingers hooked like claws; Babin going low to tackle Fargo around the legs.

Moving too swiftly for their eyes to follow, Fargo caught Pitre with a backhand to the face while simultaneously kicking Babin in the head. Both men drew away and Fargo went after Pitre. He ducked a wild swing and rammed his fist into Pitre's mouth. Blood spurted from pulped lips. A quick chop ended it.

That left Babin. He had scrambled to one side and was in a crouch. "No more, monsieur."

Fargo's dander was up. "Why should I spare you?"

"We were wrong, monsieur. And two wrongs don't make a right. Isn't that what they say?"

"There's another saying I'm fond of," Fargo said. "Maybe you've heard of it. An eye for an eye." He took a bound and planted his boot in Babin's face. Babin tried to dodge but he was too slow. Knocked flat onto his back, he held both palms out.

"I will not fight you. Beat me if you want but for me this is over."

Fargo moved to Doucet. The rooster was out to the world, blood dribbling from his mouth. "When he comes around tell him something for me."

"Let me guess. Should he lift a finger against you again, he would be wise to have a coffin made first."

"I couldn't have said it better." Fargo looked at Babin. "Get it through your heads that I might be an outsider but I was sent for. I'm here to help."

"Help do what, exactly?"

Fargo didn't answer. Instead, he wheeled and went into the tavern. Apparently no one had heard the ruckus, or if they had, they chose to ignore it. Several men had claimed his table in his absence so he stalked to the bar, and when Liana came over he asked for a bottle.

"Is something the matter?"

"Doucet."

"Not again?"

"Some idiots never learn." Fargo upended the redeye and chugged. "The good news is, he didn't spoil my mood."

"Your mood?" Liana said quizzically, and smiled. "Oh. Thank goodness. Although I have heard that men are always in the mood."

Fargo stayed at the bar. The Cajuns wanted nothing to do with him and left him alone, which suited him fine. Most left long before closing time, heading home to their wives and children. He downed half the bottle by eleven and was the last man in the tavern.

"At last I can close. It's been a long day. I need to relax."

Fargo gave her another of his hungry looks. "I know just the way."

"I bet you do." Liana stood in front of him, her breasts nearly brushing his chest. "I hope you are not all talk. I would be *très* disappointed."

Without any hint of what he was about to do, Fargo cupped her twin mounds and squeezed. Liana arched her back, her cherry lips forming a delectable O. A soft sigh issued from her throat. When she looked at him she had a hunger in her eyes to match his.

"What is good for the goose is good for the gander, *non*?"

She cupped him, low down.

Now it was Fargo's turn to go rigid with tingling pleasure. He felt her stroke him and his pole became iron. "And you said I was bold?"

"You will find that most Cajun women are not shy about their needs," Liana informed him. "When we see a man we like, we go after him."

"Do you have any sisters?"

Liana laughed, and Fargo glued his mouth to hers. His tongue met hers in a velvet swirl as he kneaded her breasts with one hand while roving his other down over her flat belly to the junction of her thighs.

Breaking the kiss, Liana stepped back. "*Non*."

For a moment Fargo thought she had been toying with him, that the whole thing was an act. "Why not?"

Liana gestured at the windows. "Someone might look in. I have a room in the back. It is most comfortable, with a nice bed. Permit me to lock up and put out the lamps."

Fargo liked the idea of a bed over the floor or a tabletop. "Whatever you want." He patted her bottom as she moved past. "I'm in no hurry. I have all night." He only hoped the man he was supposed to meet showed up. The letter had been sent six weeks ago, and the man might have changed his mind or be dead for all he knew. "Tell me. Do you know a gent by the name of Namo?"

"*Oui*. Namo Heuse," Liana answered while drawing a brocaded curtain over a window. "A good man. He lives deep in the swamp. Deeper in than anyone. He has a son named Clovis and a daughter named Halette." She looked over her shoulder, sorrow marking her features. "It is terrible, really."

"What?"

"Namo had a charming wife. I liked her a lot. Emmeline, she was called. A most capable woman. She knew the swamp and the bayous as good as anyone, and she was a good shot, but neither saved her."

"How do you mean?"

"She is one of those who have gone missing. About two months ago, now, I think it was. She left the settlement with her daughter but never made it home. Everyone joined in the search but she was never found." Liana paused. "We found Halette, though."

"Did she say what happened to her mother?"

"She told us nothing, monsieur. She was found clinging to branches high in a tree and would not say a word to her rescuers. Nor has she said a word since. The doctor says it is the shock. A pitiable sight to see her sitting in a chair, not moving, not even blinking." Liana shuddered. "She must have seen the monster. She must have seen what it did to her mother."

"How do you know a gator didn't get her?"

"Not Emmeline. She was too careful, that one. Besides, I haven't told you about the blood. At the base of the tree where they found the girl was so much blood, it sickened me to look at it."

"There must have been tracks."

"Oh, we are sure there were. But someone erased them."

"What?"

Liana was moving toward the other window. "Someone took an axe or a pick to the ground. It was chopped up, with clods of dirt everywhere. Any tracks were destroyed."

Fargo leaped to a logical conclusion. "Maybe it's a man and he was hiding the fact."

In the act of reaching for the cord, Liana shook her head. "Would the girl be in shock if it were a man? Would she be rendered mute?"

"You said there was a lot of blood."

"And you forget. Emmeline was not the first. There have been many. If a man was responsible, he would have given himself away."

Fargo wasn't so sure. "What about this Remy?"

"He has killed, yes. But as I told you, only outsiders. And only in fair fights. He doesn't murder women and children."

"How can you be so sure?"

"Trust me on this. Remy did not kill Emmeline or any of the others. You should talk to Namo. After she vanished, he refused to eat or sleep but spent every day out in his pirogue, searching."

A pirogue, as Fargo knew, was a Cajun canoe with a flat-bottomed hull, ideal for swamp use.

"Namo says he got a glimpse of the monster. It was late and he was heading home when he saw it, far off. In the dark he could not see it well, but he swears it was the size of a covered wagon."

To say Fargo was skeptical was putting it mildly. "Nothing is that big. Not even a grizzly or a buffalo."

"Namo swears to it and I believe him. You must realize. We came from Acadia and made this swamp our home. We have lived here many years now, and we know the swamp well. There are things we have seen that no one else has. Things you would not believe were I to tell you."

"Ghost and goblins," Fargo could not resist saying with a grin.

"Call them what you will. But there are more things on this earth than many of us ever dream."

Fargo would rather not insult her but it would be a cold day in hell before he let himself become *that* gullible.

Liana took a candle from behind the bar and lit the wick in the flame of the last lit lamp, then blew out the lamp. Holding the candle on high, she came over and took his hand. "Thank you for being so patient. I will try to make the wait worth your while."

"I can hardly wait."

"Might I ask why you wanted to know about Namo Heuse?"

"He's the one who sent for me. But he didn't write why."

"Surely you can guess. He must want your help in finding the creature that killed poor Emmeline." Liana glanced at him. "Who knows? Maybe you will discover that monsters and goblins are more real than you think."

4

The bedroom was every bit as comfortable as she claimed.

The bed was twice the size of most and layered in thick quilts and blankets. Embroidered pillows were propped against a mahogany headboard. Overhead was a flowered canopy with pink fringe. A plush rug covered the floor, and a dresser and a table and chair were in opposite corners.

Liana patted the top quilt. "This is my escape from the world. On Sundays I don't get up until past noon."

"Too bad tomorrow isn't Sunday," Fargo said.

"Few men ever see this room. Usually I indulge my dalliances elsewhere. You should be flattered."

Fargo moved up behind her and put his arm around her waist. "You said something about needing to relax."

Twisting her head, Liana smiled seductively. "What do you have in mind? You and your naughty thoughts."

"This," Fargo said, grinding his member against her buttocks. Right away he grew hard again. Cupping a breast, he kissed her. Liana melted into him. For the longest while their mouths and their tongues were entwined.

It was Liana who broke for breath. "Mmmm. You are a wonderful kisser. *Magnifique.*"

"You're not bad yourself." Fargo turned her so she was facing him. He kissed her neck, her throat, her ear. He sucked on the lobe and she shivered. He rimmed the ear with the tip of his tongue and she uttered a low groan.

"I am sensitive there."

Fargo took her hand and placed it on his manhood. "I'm sensitive here."

"I take the hint." Liana commenced rubbing and cupping.

Fargo could always tell women who made love a lot from women who were new to lovemaking by how they fondled him. The new ones treated his pole as if they were trying to break it in half. They were much too rough. Experienced women used a lighter touch.

Liana was experienced.

He plied her thighs and continued to tweak her breasts, switching from one to the other, feeling her nipples harden until they were like tacks. Soon she was panting, her hot breath fanning his throat as she lavished burning kisses on him.

"Clothes are nice but naked is better," Fargo said, and set to work undressing her. Fortunately she wasn't one of those females who believed in layer after layer of undergarments. No petticoats or corsets for this Cajun lady.

As Fargo shed her clothes, Liana shed his. She got his belt undone and his holster slid down his leg and thudded to the floor. His hat she tossed to the foot of the bed. Then she peeled off his shirt. "*Mon Dieu!*" she exclaimed at the sight of his whipcord torso. "So many muscles." She ran her fingers across his stomach and up over his chest. "I could eat you alive."

"Be my guest."

Fargo got her undressed and looked down, admiring her contours. She was exquisite. Her breasts were firm and full, her belly was smooth and flat, her bottom nicely rounded. Her curly thatch was silky soft to the touch. He drank her loveliness in, then got down to arousing her. First he eased her onto the bed and crawled on so he was next to her, his chest to her breasts. The quilts were so soft it was like sinking into fluff.

Liana looped an arm about his neck and pulled his

26

face down to hers. "Something tells me this will be a night I'll long remember."

"I'll try my best, ma'am."

If there was anything finer in life than a willing woman, Fargo had yet to come across it. His mouth and hands roved everywhere, exploring, arousing. She did the same. Both of them took their time, savoring the feel and the taste, her lust a mirror of his.

Eventually Fargo spread her legs wide and aligned his redwood with her slit. He ran it up and down, sparking quivers from her head to her toes. Inserting the tip, he slowly fed himself in until his steel sword was up to the hilt in her wet sheath. For a space they lay motionless on the precipice.

"I could do this forever," Liana cooed. Her eyes were hooded, her red lips more inviting than ever.

Fargo began stroking. He had experience, too, and he didn't go at her hard and fast and end it too soon. He dipped into her slowly, rocking gently on his knees, his toes braced for leverage. Her nails dug into his arms so deep, he would swear that this time she drew blood.

Finally Liana was ready. She put her mouth to his ear and whispered, "Now, amoureux. I am a flower and you are a scythe. Cut me."

Fargo had never heard it expressed quite that way before. But cut her he did, thrusting his scythe up into her flower harder and harder until the bed bounced and she cried out and arched her back and spurted.

Fargo's redwood exploded. Pinpoints of light danced before his eyes. He rocked in and out until he was spent and then sank on top of her, cushioned by her heaving bosom. But he lay there only a few moments. Rolling off to spare her his weight, he closed his eyes and drifted into sleep.

A noise awakened him.

How long he had been out, Fargo couldn't say. Beside him Liana snored, and he assumed it was her snoring that roused him. Then his gaze fell on the mirror above the table and suddenly he was fully awake, his blood racing in alarm.

The bedroom door was open. Midway between it and the bed stalked a figure with a knife in his hand. Doucet.

Fury gripped Fargo. Sheer, red-hot fury. He'd spared the fool and this was how Doucet repaid him. As yet, Doucet hadn't realized he was awake. Fargo remedied that. Abruptly rolling, he deliberately fell over the side of the bed. He landed next to his gun belt and molded the Colt to his palm. He thought Doucet would come around after him and he would blow the Cajun to kingdom come. But there was a gasp, and then nothing. He sat up.

Doucet was on his knees on the bed, his blade to Liana's throat. Grinning smugly, he said, "We meet again."

"For the last time."

"I agree." Doucet's eyes glittered. "You will drop your revolver or I will cut her."

Liana's own eyes reflected mute appeal. She started to move but Doucet grabbed her hair and wrenched her head back, further exposing her throat.

"Don't move, *ma chère*. I do not want to harm you. But you have brought this on yourself by sleeping with this pig."

"Where are your friends?" Fargo asked.

"Pitre and Babin refused to help. They said I should let it drop. That you had proven the better man." Doucet swore. "They said that to *me*. As if the likes of you could ever be *my* better."

"Let her go. This is between you and me."

"No."

"Then all your talk about caring for her was a lie." Fargo tensed his legs for his push off the floor.

"To the contrary. But a man does what he must. Now you will drop that revolver as I have told you or she bleeds. Do you want her death on your conscience?"

"I'd rather have your brains splattered all over a wall. But you win." Fargo let the Colt fall.

"Excellent. Now stand up."

"Whatever you want. Just don't hurt her." Fargo put both hands flat and began to rise. His right hand was only inches from the Colt. He didn't glance down at it, though. That would give him away.

"Most excellent," Doucet gloated. Then he did something Fargo didn't expect: he ducked behind Liana so that only part of his face was visible, a cheek and one eye. "Nice and slow, yes?"

Fargo kept on rising but he didn't snatch up the Colt as he intended. He needed to be sure. There must be no risk to Liana. His pants slid down around his ankles, bunching about his boots.

"Hold your arms out from your sides," Doucet commanded, "and back up until you are against the far wall."

Reluctantly, Fargo complied.

Only then did Doucet slide off the bed and step away from Liana. He shoved her as he did, growling, "Stay on that bed, woman." A few quick steps brought him to the Colt, which he picked up and cocked.

"How dare you lay a hand on me!" Liana fumed, rising on her elbows. "I will tell everyone what you have done."

"Go right ahead. You haven't been harmed. As for this outsider—" and he gestured with the Colt at Fargo—"no one will care what I do to him."

"The person who sent for him will."

"So he claims. But he hasn't said who it was, or why." Doucet shook his head. "No one will care that another outsider became lost in the swamp and was never heard from again. Or that is the story we will tell if anyone should come looking for him."

Liana glanced worriedly at Fargo then softened her tone toward Doucet. "Please. I ask you nicely. Don't harm him. We have been friendly, have we not? Spare him as a favor to me?"

"True, we have been friends," Doucet said. "Until the moment you slept with this pig. Now I no longer care if you live or die."

"Damn you."

Doucet laughed and addressed Fargo. "Women. *Ce n'est pas la peine. N'est-ce pas?*" When Fargo didn't answer, he translated, "They are not worth the trouble. Isn't that right?"

"You are the pig here," Liana said.

"How soon they turn on us, eh?" Doucet went on addressing Fargo. "One day they hold our hand and go for a walk with us, and the next they glare at us and call us pigs."

"I want you out of my room, out of my tavern, out of my life."

"What you want, my dear, and what will happen, are two different things." Doucet pointed the Colt at Fargo's chest. "The question now is whether I kill you outright or have fun with you a while."

"No, Doucet, please," Liana said.

"Shut up. Another word out of you, just one, and I swear I will shoot him. Not to kill, mind you. I want him to suffer. I'll shoot him in the knee, perhaps. Or in that tool of his he used on you." Doucet glanced down. "*Mon Dieu.* That I should be so endowed."

Fargo had stayed silent long enough. To keep the Cajun's tongue wagging he revealed, "The gent who sent for me is called Namo Heuse. Maybe you've heard of him."

Doucet's brow puckered. "Namo? *Oui.* I know him well. But what would he want with an outsider?"

"He sent me a letter by way of the army. I work for them at times. I scout. I track. The letter doesn't say exactly why he wanted me to come. Only that he needs my help to avenge the death of someone he loved."

Liana sat up on the bed. "*Je comprends.* You know about Namo's wife, Doucet. I think Namo wants him to track the thing that killed Emmeline."

Doucet glared at her. "I told you to be quiet, remember?" To Fargo he said, "Namo is a good man but he's a fool. This isn't the prairie. The swamp and bayous are mostly water and nothing leaves tracks in water."

Fargo shrugged. "I reckon he figures I can help him."

"He will be disappointed, then, that I had to kill you for the sake of my honor."

"No!" Liana cried. "Think, Doucet. For once in your life don't let your temper get the better of you. Think of how many people have gone missing. Think of how many the monster has killed. And it will go on killing unless it's stopped." She slid to the edge of the bed. "Perhaps you are right and this man can't help us. But what if he can? What if he can put a stop to the killings? Think of all the lives that will be saved. *Cajun* lives."

Doucet didn't say anything.

"You speak of your honor. But it was you who started this. No one will think highly of you for murdering him. But they *will* think highly of you if you spare him. You have him at your mercy. But let him live for the good of our people. Show that you have true honor."

Lowering the Colt, Doucet gnawed on his lower lip.

"Spare him, and I won't hold this against you," Liana went on trying to persuade him. "You and I will still be friends. You will still be welcome here."

"I don't know," Doucet said uncertainly. "You might forgive me but he certainly won't."

"How about that, Skye?" Liana asked. "He hasn't harmed you. Are you willing to let bygones be bygones?"

Fargo didn't see where he had much of a choice. "How do I know I won't end up with his blade in my back?"

"Doucet isn't a coward," Liana said. "When he kills you, he will be facing you."

Doucet looked at her and the suggestion of a smile curled his lips. "I thank you for that. And I have given it thought. You are right. Our people must come first."

He backed to the doorway and when he reached it he set the Colt on the floor. "I spare you, outsider. But hear this. Watch what you say and what you do. Insult me or my people again and I will not forgive. *Comprenez-vous?*" He didn't wait for an answer but wheeled and was gone.

"Well," Fargo said, lowering his arms. "That didn't end like I thought it would."

Liana sank back in relief on the pillows. "You don't know how close you came."

"Oh, I think I do," Fargo said. Hiking his pants so he could walk, he sat next to her. "I have you to thank."

A playful twinkle came into her eyes. "And how will you go about thanking me, monsieur?"

Fargo grinned and reached for her.

5

Fargo never did like being stared at, and by five o'clock the next day he'd had a bellyful.

The tavern filled up by noon. So many Cajuns, they were shoulder to shoulder and wall to wall. So many men, they were three and four deep at the bar and every table was filled. All there because of him.

Word had spread rapidly. The swamp grapevine, Liana called it. News that an outsider had arrived at the tavern, and that he was there to meet one of their own. The outsider was a famous scout, the rumor went, a tracker whose skills were often called on by the army. And he had come to the Atchafalaya Swamp to solve the mystery of the vanishings.

Small wonder, then, that the tavern was packed.

Fargo had a corner table to himself. He drank and played solitaire and grew tired of the endless stares and fingers jabbed in his direction. His mood wasn't helped any by the presence of Doucet, who swaggered around as if he were somebody important.

"I am sorry," Liana said at one point as she was refilling Fargo's glass to the brim with her best whiskey. "I never expected this."

"Makes two of us."

Liana bent so her mouth was close to his ear. "I am also sorry about Doucet."

"Why? What is he up to?" As if Fargo couldn't guess.

"He is going around telling everyone how he clashed with you over me," Liana related. "And how for the good of everyone, and out of the nobleness of his heart, he spared you."

"Leave the bottle."

"Don't let him get to you. He loves to hear himself talk. Most will know there must be more to his story."

"Leave the bottle anyway."

The afternoon dragged. By three Fargo was wondering if Namo would show. By four he was willing to bet Namo wouldn't. By five he was so tired of being stared at that he was about to get up and go for a walk when the door opened and in came a man holding a small girl in his arms. A boy of twelve or so trailed after them. Instantly the tavern fell quiet, completely, utterly silent. No one talked. No one whispered. No one so much as breathed loud.

The man holding the girl was rake thin but all sinew. He sported a clipped beard much like Fargo's. He paused and surveyed the room from end to end.

The boy said something to him and they threaded through the throng toward the corner table.

"You are the only outsider here so you must be him."

"And you must be Namo Heuse, the gent who wrote to me." Fargo introduced himself.

The rake-thin Cajun said quietly, "I wasn't sure you would come. I wasn't even sure you got my letter. Then I got your reply, and here I am."

"I have a fair idea of why you wrote to me," Fargo said. "But there's one thing I don't know. Why *me*?"

"I read about you in the New Orleans newspaper. About the time you tracked some killers in Missouri and saved a woman's life. The paper said the army considers you the best tracker and scout alive. It said you can find anyone or anything, anywhere, anytime."

"Don't believe everything you read."

Namo pulled out a chair and set his daughter down. "This is Halette."

"How do you do," Fargo said.

The girl sat ramrod straight, her cherub face blank, her hazel eyes fixed unblinkingly on the wall.

Namo sadly frowned. "She hasn't spoken a word

34

since her mother disappeared. All she does is sit and stare. I've taken her to a doctor and two healers but they are unable to help. They say she might come out of it with time but there's no telling when." Namo indicated the boy. "And this is Clovis. Don't let his age fool you. He's a good hunter. He's killed just about everything that walks, crawls and flies in the Atchafalaya."

"That's a lot of killing."

Namo pulled out the chair next to his daughter and sat. "You say you have some idea of why I sent for you? I take it, then, you've heard about my wife, my sweet Emmeline."

"Her and the others who have disappeared, yes."

"Disappeared, nothing. They were killed by a swamp beast. I know. I've seen it with my own eyes."

"If you were able to get that close on your own, why send for me?" Fargo wanted to know.

"You don't understand. I've hunted it every day since my wife vanished. Every day from dawn until dusk for the past two months. Sixty days, and all I have to show for it is that one glimpse. Only for a second or two, with night about to fall."

"What do you think it was?"

Namo hesitated. "I'm not sure. I know what it wasn't. It wasn't an alligator and it wasn't a bear. It wasn't a cougar or a bobcat. It was much too big."

"And now you want me to find it for you?"

"No. I want you to help *me* find it. But first I want your word that you won't kill it when we do. Leave that to me."

Fargo was taking the measure of this man as they talked, and he liked what he saw. Namo wasn't foaming at the mouth with rage; the Cajun had thought this out and knew exactly what he was doing. "In your letter you mentioned a thousand dollars."

"All the money I have, yes. And it is yours if you agree to help."

"Let's say I do. I can't stick around forever. I can stay a month. Not much more."

"I will take what I can get."

"And what if we don't find it? What if I try my best and I don't have any more luck than you've had?"

"You will still get your money. Half today and the rest when you decide you have had enough."

Fargo started to extend his arm to shake on the deal.

"We can start in the morning. Clovis and Halette won't be any bother, I assure you."

"Wait. You're taking your kids along?"

"*Oui*. I can't leave them home alone. Not with Halette as she is."

Fargo studied the man more closely. "They'd be safer in your cabin than out in the swamp with us."

"I disagree. And they are my children. It is my decision."

Fargo withdrew his hand and sat back. "I don't know as I like it."

"You're having second thoughts?"

"Third and fourth thoughts," Fargo responded. "I won't deny I can use the money. It will buy me a week or two of poker and women in St. Jo. But I don't need it so bad that I'll agree to going after this so-called monster with your kids along."

Namo Heuse frowned. He glanced at his daughter and then at his son and drummed his fingers on the table. "How can I make you understand? I love them. I love them more than anything. I've already lost their mother and I couldn't bear to lose them, too."

"Then leave them at home." Fargo had an inspiration. "Better yet, leave them with relatives. Or with friends here in the settlement."

"I wouldn't want to impose on anyone in Gros Ville."

"Now you're just making excuses." Fargo gestured at the bar. "Liana might do it. She's been real friendly to me."

"I can't let my daughter out of my sight."

"Then hunt the thing yourself." Fargo considered

that the end of the matter. "I'll take twenty dollars for my expenses and we'll call it even."

Namo Heuse put his hand on Halette's shoulder. "Look at her. Look at how she is. Now watch." He pushed back his chair, got up, and made for the bar. Barely had he taken half a dozen steps when Halette began to tremble and to whimper. She didn't turn her head to see where he had gone. She just sat there whimpering.

Her brother, Clovis, bowed his head.

Namo turned around and came back. Reclaiming his seat, he gave his daughter's arm a tender squeeze. "She does that every time I leave her side. She doesn't talk. She doesn't cry. She just makes that sound."

Fargo took a long swallow of whiskey. "It's too dangerous in the swamp. You're taking too great a risk."

"Do you think I don't know that?" Namo rubbed a hand across his face, and only then did Fargo realize how bone weary the man was. It showed in the deep lines and in his haunted eyes. "But what choice do I have? I must find the thing. I must kill it. Or never again hold my head high as a man should."

"But the danger," Fargo persisted.

"Clovis is old enough. He understands the risks And Emmeline was his mother. As for Halette—" Namo regarded his daughter with the undeniable love of a devoted father. "You see what happens when I leave her. The doctor says she could have fits if I am away too long. Convulsions, he called them. He said they could kill her. You talk about risks? I don't dare leave her alone."

"Damn."

"Yes. Damn. What is the saying, monsieur? I am caught between a rock and a hard place. Between the love I had for my wife and the love I bear for my child." Namo paused. "I've never done what I am about to do. I have always been too proud. But I will do it now. I will beg you."

"Don't," Fargo said.

"I plead with you to help me. I can't do it alone. Not and watch over my children, both."

"Damn, damn, damn, damn, damn."

"You are weakening? Good. I beg you on my dead wife's behalf. They say you are one of the best at what you do. Only a few are your equal. Jim Bridger, but he is old. Kit Carson, but I couldn't find out where he is. And that mountain man in the Rockies who has a Shoshone wife but he never leaves the Rockies. So that left you."

"If I had known about your kids, I'd never have come."

"You hate children that much?"

"I hate seeing them die." Fargo remembered one little girl in particular. He had been fond of her, and she died in his arms.

"With the two of us working together, maybe they won't."

"Maybe," Fargo said.

"I will go anyway, you know. With or without you, I will continue to hunt the creature. And they will continue to go with me."

"I should hit you with a chair."

Namo Heuse grinned. "You've changed your mind. But let me hear you say the words."

"By any chance are you related to Doucet?"

"Why would you ask such a thing? He and I are nothing alike."

"You're both bastards." Fargo smiled as he said it. "All right, Namo. I'll do as you want. We'll take your son and your daughter." He looked at them. "God help us."

"Thank you."

"Save it for after. If we're still alive." Fargo nodded at the kids. "And if they are."

"We can head out at dawn. I came by pirogue. It is faster than walking. And safer."

"I have a horse."

"Where we are going is not for horses, monsieur. You must leave the animal here."

"That's my point. There's no stable or livery."

But there was Liana, and when Fargo asked, she agreed to let Fargo tie the stallion out behind the tavern, and promised to feed and water him while Fargo was gone.

"For you, handsome. But only for you. And be careful out there, yes? The swamp is a very dangerous place."

Fargo had no need to be reminded. But he shut it from his mind for the time being, in part because she invited him to stay with her a second night if he wished. Of course he wished. While he waited for her to close, he went out for some air. Night had fallen over the Atchafalaya. From the swamp came bellows and croaks and an occasional roar.

Fargo had been in swamps before. There were no more treacherous places on earth. They were home to a host of things that could do a man in. The prairie and the mountains had their perils but compared to a swamp they were downright hospitable. He could never live there. Not that he shied from danger. He just wasn't fond of snakes and even less of quicksand, and he had a passionate dislike for mosquitoes. And, too, he preferred to have a horse under him, not a canoe.

Far off something screamed. A death shriek, unless Fargo was mistaken. Prey had fallen to a predator. He thought of the animal they were going after. He didn't buy that nonsense about a monster. There must be a logical explanation. Whatever the creature was, if it was flesh and blood it could be killed. All he needed to do was get it in his gun sights.

"Mister?"

Fargo nearly jumped, and cursed himself for his nerves. He turned, surprised to find Clovis Heuse. "Does your father want to see me?"

"No. I came looking for you myself. It's him I want to talk about, though."

"I'm listening."

"Don't let anything happen to him. Losing our mother

39

was awful enough. We couldn't stand to lose him, too."

"I'll do my best but I can't make any promises."

The boy didn't seem to hear him. "I'd take it poorly if he died. I might even blame you. Something to keep in mind." Without so much as a "good night," he wheeled and walked off.

Fargo stared after him in disbelief. Was it his imagination or had he just been threatened?

6

The stillness was what got to you.

Whole stretches of the swamp were as still as a cemetery. Moss-covered cypress reared in rows like headstones, their branchcs bowed as if they were about to pounce on the unwary. Willow trees hung their branches as if weeping for the fallen. Shadow and gloom held sway even in the bright of day.

The wildlife seemed to have been sucked into the muck and the ooze. Nary a bird chirped. Even the insects were quiet.

Fargo was glad when they came to a bayou. The open channel was a relief after the murk. It felt good to have the sun on his face. He stroked his paddle, matching his rhythm to the Cajun's.

Between them perched Clovis and Halette. The girl sat facing Fargo, not her father, her face vacant, her eyes pits of emptiness. Now and again Fargo would glance at her and for a few fleeting seconds he caught a glimmer of—something. When that happened he made it a point to smile but she never smiled back.

Clovis sat with a rifle across his legs. For twelve years old he was a remarkable shot, as he'd demonstrated when a large cottonmouth glided toward them and he put a slug smack in its eye when it was still a good twenty feet away.

"Nice shooting," Fargo had complimented him.

"Shucks, mister. That wasn't anything."

"Don't brag, boy," Namo said over his shoulder. "It's not seemly."

Now, as they moved at a brisk pace along the winding

bayou, Fargo thought to ask, "Where are we headed? You haven't told me."

"To where I saw the beast. It's far into the Atchafalaya, further than most ever go."

"What makes you think the thing is still there?"

Namo's arms pumped with effortless ease. "I noticed a pattern. One or two would go missing and everything was fine for a month or so. Then more would disappear, and it was fine for a while."

Fargo put two and two together. "You think the thing has a territory it roams, like a bear or a cougar?"

"That would explain a lot, yes."

"But what it doesn't explain is what the thing is and where it came from and why it's attacking people," Fargo said. Most animals avoid humans if they can help it.

"I have an idea what it is but I don't want to say anything until I'm sure. And if I'm right, we will be in for the fight of our lives."

"Don't forget your kids," Fargo said with just enough resentment to let Namo know he was still angry.

"They'll be fine. You've seen Clovis shoot."

Fargo looked at the children and again caught a gleam in Halette's eyes. But the next moment the blank look came over her again. "What are you playing at?" he quietly asked.

"What was that?" From Namo.

"I was talking to myself." Fargo didn't want to get the man's hopes up, only to have them dashed.

For over a mile they relied on the bayou. Presently, though, Namo veered into a tributary, which in turn merged into the swamp and once again they glided through brackish water so dark Fargo couldn't see the bottom. Twice he spotted alligators. The first, a small one, dived out of sight. The second, almost as long as their pirogue, stared balefully from atop a hummock where it was sprawled in reptilian ease.

"We'll see a lot more," Namo let him know.

"I can't wait."

The change from day to night was abrupt. What light there was didn't gradually fade. One moment the swamp was its perpetual gray, the next they were plunged in black.

"We should stop," Fargo suggested.

"I can go another hour yet."

Fargo didn't see how, not when he couldn't see the other end of the pirogue from where he sat. It invited disaster. Night was when all the gators were abroad. And there would be no warning if they came on a poisonous snake. "What about your kids?"

"For them we stop."

After they pulled their craft onto a small island, Namo gathered wood for the fire and got it going using a fire steel and flint. On his hands and knees, he puffed tiny fingers of flame to crackling life.

Clovis had shot a squirrel shortly before the sun went down so supper consisted of coffee and squirrel stew. The boy skinned it and chopped the meat and didn't care one whit that his hands were covered with gore.

Fargo ate with relish. He wasn't fussy when it came to food. Cook it well, and he would eat just about anything. He was on his second helping and had just set his coffee cup at his feet when loud crashing broke out across a narrow span that separated their island from another.

"Deer," Namo said. "They caught our scent and ran off."

Clovis came around the fire and held his rifle out to Fargo. "Want to look at it? It was my mother's. We found it where she died and Papa gave it to me."

It was an old Sharps. Somewhere or other the stock had cracked and been wound with strips of leather. Fargo pressed it to his shoulder and sighted down the long barrel. "Nice gun."

"Have you ever fired a Sharps, monsieur? They kick."

"I owned one," Fargo enlightened him. For years, until he switched. There were days when he thought about switching back again.

Clovis gazed with interest at the Henry propped against Fargo's leg. "Why did you give it up? A Sharps will drop just about anything."

"That it will," Fargo agreed. But the Sharps was a single-shot rifle. The Henry held fifteen rounds in a tubular magazine and another in the chamber. Someone once joked that you could load it on Sunday and fire it all week. "But there are times when I need to spray a lot of lead."

"Such as when?"

"Oh, when a war party is after your scalp and there are five or ten of them and only one of you." Fargo gave the Sharps back and said fondly, "But I've dropped many a buff and many a griz with one of these."

"When I am older I will go to Texas and shoot some buffalo," Clovis said. "I have always wanted to do that and we do not have any in Louisiana. No grizzlies, either."

"Count your blessings."

"I'm not afraid of them." Clovis patted his Sharps. "Not so long as I have this."

"A lot of people are afraid of the monster, as they call it," Fargo remarked.

"Not me. I hate it. I want it dead for what it did to my mama. I don't care what it is or how big it is. When we find it, my Sharps will kill it."

"What is this 'we'?" Namo broke in. "You will protect your sister like I told you and leave the shooting to me." He caught himself. "And to Monsieur Fargo, of course."

"Of course," Fargo echoed. But to tell the truth, he still didn't see why Namo needed him. The Cajun knew the swamp better than he ever could.

"I have been meaning to ask," Namo said. "Is it true you shot the biggest grizzly ever killed?"

"Where did you hear that?"

"I read it somewhere."

"You read wrong. The few grizzlies I've shot were big but nowhere near the biggest. I think you've got me confused with a mountain man who supposedly shot a griz the size of a cabin."

"Then it wasn't you?"

"I just said it wasn't."

"Oh."

Fargo suspected that Namo thought the "monster" was a giant bear. So Namo had sent for someone he mistakenly thought to be a killer of giant bears. It gave him something to ponder as he lay on his back with his head on his laced fingers, gazing up at the star-speckled firmament.

The next day was more of the same. The vastness of the swamp amazed him. As big as a small state, it seemed. So big, the Atchafalaya had never been fully explored. Vast tracts had never felt the tread of a human foot. White feet, anyway. Namo mentioned that several small tribes lived so deep in the swamp, whites rarely saw them.

Which reminded Fargo of something. "What can you tell me about the Mad Indian?"

Without breaking his rhythm paddling, Namo answered, "Not much. I've never seen him but I've heard the stories. I came on one of his camps once, the day after he had been there."

"How do you know the camp was his?"

"I heard him laugh. He must have heard me and got out of there."

"His laugh?"

"You will know it when you hear it. It is not a laugh you forget. It is madness given sound, and why he is called the Mad Indian."

"What does he do besides laugh at people?"

"He sets snares for rabbits. He has been seen taking them from the snares."

"So he laughs and likes rabbit meat? He doesn't sound very dangerous to me."

"He has also been seen a few times near where

45

people have vanished. No one can say for sure he had a hand in it, but it is interesting, don't you think?"

"Interesting," Fargo agreed. "What tribe is he from?"

"No one can say. You must understand. Here in the swamp and along the coast are many tribes that want nothing to do with whites. Tribes we do not even know the names of. Exactly how many, no one can say. It could be the Mad Indian is from one of them."

"There are a lot of 'could be's about this."

"*Oui*, from your point of view I guess there are."

Fargo glanced at Halette. She was facing him, as she always did. For an instant he detected a glint of something in her eyes, or thought he did, but then her gaze became as blank as ever and he questioned whether he had really seen it.

The deeper they traveled into the swamp, the more alligators and snakes they saw. And that was not all. The swamp was home to a host of creatures that crept and crawled and bit and clawed. In the evening, swarms of mosquitoes besieged them. Leeches were a problem, and once a snapping turtle nearly took off Fargo's fingers. The stifling muggy heat, the bogs and the quicksand—why anyone would want to live in a swamp, Fargo would never know.

Yet it had its beauty, too, such as occasional clear pools, sparkling gems in the maze of muck and mire. Gorgeous flowers, the likes of which Fargo had never seen and couldn't peg a name to. Birds with brilliant plumage. Lizards at home in the trees as well as on the ground. Spiders as big as Fargo's hand. Now and then he spied large cranes, often standing on one leg.

Fargo grew to like the Spanish moss that draped the cypress and oaks. Much of the vegetation was so unlike the vegetation of the prairie and mountains that it was like being in a whole new world. At night the thick growth added to the swamp's sinister atmosphere.

Still, it was the wild, and Fargo loved wild places of any kind. He drank in so much that was new. But he never for a moment forgot the dangers. He was always alert for snakes, always wary of alligators.

On the afternoon of the fourth day they came to a narrow channel of clear water.

"Where did this come from?" Fargo asked.

"The swamp is not all swamp."

The Cajun stuck to the channel until a lightning-blasted tree appeared on the right bank. "This way," he said, and struck off into more moss-ridden ranks of cypress.

Fargo was impressed at how confidently Namo found his way around. So much of the swamp looked exactly like so much else that it took long familiarity with the byways and landmarks to navigate with certainty.

They managed another mile before the sun rested on the rim of the world. The Cajun gazed to the west, frowned, and urged, "Paddle faster! There is a spot we must reach before dark."

That spot turned out to be a broad hummock surprisingly thin of trees and growth. They hauled the pirogue from the water and walked over to the charred remains of a fire.

Namo pointed. "That is where I saw it."

All Fargo saw was swamp and more swamp. The thing could be anywhere—if there even was a thing—but he held his peace. He chopped a tree for firewood and when he brought the last armload, supper was ready. Clovis had killed a snake and Namo had cut off the head and the tail and skinned it.

Fargo wasn't all that fond of snake meat. He'd eaten it before, but it wasn't one of his favorites. "What kind of snake was this?"

Namo thought a bit. "I don't know as there is a word in English for it, *mon ami*. It is said the swamp is home to over a thousand and most are not known to anyone but those of us who live here."

Fargo picked at the meat. Afterward they sat around making small talk. Toward midnight he lay down. His stomach growled and he willed it not to.

So what if he was still hungry? It was no great inconvenience.

They were to take turns keeping watch, as always. Namo wanted Clovis to take the first turn and Fargo said it was fine by him.

The swamp was alive with noise. There was the usual riot of croaks and bellows and occasional roars and screeches, and as always, the insects.

Fargo started to drift off. He was on the cusp of slumber when a hand fell on his shoulder and shook him.

"Wake up, monsieur!"

"What is it?" Fargo rose onto his elbows.

Namo was on his feet with his rifle in his hands. Little Halette had sat up and was peering fearfully into the dark.

"Listen," Clovis whispered.

Fargo heard, and his skin crawled.

7

From out of the dark heart of the swamp it wafted, an eerie cry, part shriek and part squeal. It went from a low pitch to a high screech and seemed to pulse and throb in the very air. Every other creature fell silent— the frogs, the alligators, even the bugs. The night was completely still save for the bellow of the beast.

"Mon Dieu!" Namo Heuse exclaimed.

Clovis let out a gasp.

As for Halette, she had one hand pressed to her throat and the other to her mouth. Her eyes were wide and she cast about as if she intended to flee.

"Stay calm, child," Namo said. "The monster is far from here. It can't harm us."

Halette erupted into motion. But she didn't run toward her father or her brother. She flew at Fargo and before he could gather his wits, she wrapped her arms around his legs and broke into loud sobs.

"We're safe. Don't worry." Fargo patted her shoulder, not knowing what else to do.

Either Halette didn't hear him or she didn't believe him because she cried all the harder.

The other cry, the cry out of the swamp, faded. But it left the short hairs at the nape of Fargo's neck prickling. Whatever made it had to be huge, exactly as the Cajun claimed.

As if Namo could read Fargo's thoughts, he asked in breathless amazement, "Do you believe me now, *mon ami*?"

"I believe you," Fargo said, adding, "One thing is for sure. That was no bear." He looked down at the girl, who was still weeping and quaking. "Shouldn't you do something?"

"Oh. *Pardon*." Namo came over and began prying Halette's fingers loose. She resisted, clinging to Fargo as a drowning child would cling to a floating log, but at last Namo succeeded and scooped her into his arms. "*Ne vous en faites pas*. I am here, daughter."

Clovis was staring anxiously into the swamp. "What was that, Papa? What can make such a sound?"

Strangely, Fargo had the feeling he had heard something like it before but he couldn't recollect exactly when or where.

"I don't know what it is, nor do I care," Namo was saying. "All that matters is it killed your mother. The three of us will not rest until we have avenged her."

Fargo wondered if Namo included him or Halette in that "three." "Whatever it is, you were right. It's a long way off."

"But will it stay a long way? I hope not. I hope it comes for us. Right now. Right here."

"We shouldn't have brought your kids."

Namo snorted in annoyance. "We have been all through that. They are here and that is that." He carried Halette to her blankets and laid her on her side. "I propose we get some sleep while we can. Morning will come too soon."

Fargo tried but it was pretty near hopeless. He tossed. He turned. He stared at the stars. He peered into the moss-shrouded Atchafalaya. Eventually his eyelids grew heavy. He was on the verge of falling asleep when a screech rent the night. So loud and so close, it seemed to come from right next to him. Pushing up into a crouch, he grabbed the Henry.

Clovis was by the fire, terror-struck.

"It's here!" Namo shouted, rising, only to have his daughter do as she had done to Fargo and wrap her arms around his legs.

There was a commotion in the swamp. Fargo swung around but all he saw was the black of the pit. The starlight wasn't strong enough to penetrate the thick canopy.

"Do you hear that?" Clovis whispered.

Fargo's gut balled into a knot. For from the blackness came *breathing*. Heavy, laborious, as if the act of working its lungs was an exertion. Grizzly bears wheezed like that, only not as loud.

"It's watching us!" Namo said.

Clovis flung limbs on the fire. The flames leapt high, and the ring of light grew. But only by a dozen feet. Not nearly enough to relieve the blackness, or to show them the creature.

"Why doesn't it do something?" Namo wondered.

Fargo edged forward. He wanted to see it. Just a glimpse, enough to tell what it was.

"Careful, monsieur," Clovis warned.

Something stirred in the water but it was only a snake gliding swiftly away.

Fargo had the Henry to his cheek. He took another step, straining his eyes for all they were worth. The moss lent form where there wasn't any, lent substance to empty space. "Where are you?" he said under his breath.

The next moment the swamp exploded with racket, with tremendous splashing and the snap and crackle of brush.

For a few heartbeats Fargo saw a vague shape. There was the suggestion of enormous bulk. For its size it was incredibly quick. It was there one second, gone the next. The thing plowed through the heavy growth without hindrance, the sounds growing fainter and fainter until once again, the night was quiet.

"Thank God!" Clovis exclaimed.

Fargo shared the sentiment. Whatever that thing was, if it had attacked, he doubted they could bring it down. Not in the dark. Not as huge as it was. The breath of death had brushed them and gone by.

Namo, however, was filled with rage. Shaking a fist, he hollered, "Come back here! Face us, beast!"

"Don't press our luck," Fargo advised.

"I want it dead. I want it dead more than I have ever wanted anything."

Halette had stopped sobbing and was on her knees, her thin arms wrapped tight, trembling like a leaf in a gale. Namo didn't notice. He stormed toward the water, shaking his fist and blistering the air.

"Père!" Clovis shouted, and ran after him.

Smothering curses of his own, Fargo squatted. He touched Halette's hair, saying, "It's gone. We're safe. Don't worry." He twisted to yell for Namo to come back.

"No one is ever safe."

Fargo looked at her, at her upturned faced streaked with tears, at her quivering lips. "You can talk."

"I have been me for a while now," Halette said softly. "I just had nothing to say."

"I should tell your father." Fargo cupped a hand to his mouth.

"Non! Not yet. Please." Halette put her small hand on his. "You must help me, monsieur. Make him see we must leave this awful place or all of us will end up like my *mère.*"

Fargo leaned toward her. "They tell me you saw what happened. You saw what killed her."

"Oui."

"If it won't upset you, I'd like to hear."

The girl bowed her head, and shook. "You ask a lot."

"I came a long way to help your pa, girl. The least you can do is help me. If I know what it is, I'll know what to do."

Halette began reciting in a tiny, scared voice. "It was awful. My mama had me climb a tree. She said I would be safe up near the top. I did as she wanted. It was dark, so very dark, and I couldn't see much." She stopped.

Fargo waited. Let her tell it in her own good time.

"Then it came, monsieur. It was big, so big. My mother shot her rifle but it did no good. I heard"— Halette stopped and sucked in a breath—"I heard her screams—"

"That's enough. So you don't know what it is?"

"I know only that it is not like anything I have ever seen or heard. They call it a monster, and it is."

"You were scared. It was dark."

Fargo slowly rose and she rose with him.

"My mother couldn't kill it and she was a good shot. You can't kill it. Nor can Papa." Halette clutched at his buckskins. "We must go back. Make Papa go back too. Before it is too late."

Just then Namo and Clovis returned. Seeing Halette, Namo bellowed for joy and swept her into his arms. Clovis, too, was delighted, and spun in circles, whooping. Both had forgotten the beast.

But not Fargo. He made a circuit of the hummock. Some frogs croaked and a gator grunted but the rest of the swamp was unnaturally still. He thought he heard, faint in the distance, the breaking of underbrush, but he couldn't be sure. He was turning to go back when he heard a sound he *was* sure about: the splashing of a paddle. Dropping onto a knee, he spied what he took to be a pirogue gliding toward the hummock. But as it came closer he saw that it was a canoe.

A silhouette told him only one person was in it. A Cajun, or so Fargo reckoned until the canoe was near enough for him to see that the man was naked from the waist up and had hair that spilled past his shoulders. Fargo saw him put down the paddle and pick up a curved pole and a short stick. Belatedly, Fargo realized what they were: a bow and arrow. The man was about to loose a shaft at the Heuses.

By then the canoe was only a few yards from the hummock. Setting down the Henry, Fargo took a long leap and launched himself from shore. The warrior cried out in surprise as Fargo slammed into him. The canoe tilted from the impact and down they went. Rank swamp water embraced them.

Fargo got hold of a wrist and kicked to the surface. To his surprise, the warrior offered no resistance. Hauling him onto dry land, Fargo let go and retrieved the Henry.

The Indian looked up, his long hair hiding much of

his face. But Fargo could tell he was old, very old, and his body much more frail than it had appeared at first. The man wore a breechclout and nothing else. His legs were spindly, his knees knobby. Each of his ribs stood out as if his skin were too tight. The effect was that of a walking skeleton.

"Who are you?"

An odd sort of laugh was the reply. The Indian pushed his hair aside, revealing a swarthy face seamed with wrinkles. So many wrinkles, he had to be eighty if he was a day. His dark eyes glittered and he bared his teeth in a mocking grin.

"You're the one they call the Mad Indian."

"So the white dogs say," the man said, and cackled. "What will you do now that you have caught me?" And he laughed again.

"I'm not your enemy."

"All whites are my enemies. I will hate your kind until the day I die."

"Why? What did whites ever do to you? And where did you learn to speak the white tongue?"

The Mad Indian pushed up off the ground, his bony fists clenched, his teeth bared. "What did the whites do? *What did they do?*" he practically screamed.

From over by the fire Namo Heuse yelled, "Fargo, is someone with you? What is going on?"

The Mad Indian glared at the Cajuns and then at Fargo. "By the words of the black robes will you die! An eye for an eye, they told my people! An eye for an eye and a tooth for a tooth!"

"The black robes?" Fargo repeated. "Do you mean priests?"

The old man threw his head back and howled with vicious hate. "Black robes! Black robes! Black robes!" he cried while hopping up and down, first on one foot and then the other.

"What the hell?"

The Mad Indian pointed a gnarled finger at Fargo's chest. "It kills you! It kills you and I am happy! What do you think of that, white dog?"

"No wonder they call you mad."

"Mad?" the old Indian said, and did more prancing. "Mad, mad, mad, mad, mad!"

Namo and Clovis were running toward them, Namo with Halette in his arms. "Who is that, Fargo?"

"The local lunatic."

Suddenly the Mad Indian whirled and sprang to his canoe. With unexpected speed he swung up and over the gunwale, scooped up the paddle from the bottom, and commenced a flurry of backstrokes. "Mad, mad, mad, mad, mad!" he tittered insanely.

Namo came to a stop. "It's him! The Mad Indian!"

"If he were any madder he'd be rabid."

"Shoot him!" Clovis urged.

"What for?" Fargo wasn't about to kill an unarmed old man whose only offense, if it could be called that, was that he was completely out of his mind.

The canoe was twenty feet out and still retreating. Another cackle mocked them, along with, "All of you will die! You'll see! This is his swamp, not yours! He has come from the time before to slay and punish!"

"What is he talking about?" Clovis asked.

"Beats the hell out of me."

The canoe and its crazed occupant melted into the ink and the moss. The lapping of the paddle faded.

"First the monster, then the Mad Indian," Namo said. "It must be true, what people say, that the two are linked."

"How can that be, *mon père*?"

"I don't know, son."

Nor did Fargo, but he did have an idea about something else. "It was the fire," he remarked.

"What was?"

"The reason the monster, as you call it, didn't attack us. I suspect it was afraid of the fire."

Namo grinned excitedly. "If that is the case, we can use fire to trap it and kill it."

"If it doesn't kill us first," Clovis said.

8

Four days they searched. Four days of stifling heat and awful humidity. Four days of bugs and more bugs. Four days of always being on the watch for snakes and gators. Four long, exhausting days, and at the end of the fourth day they had nothing to show for it.

"Not a sign anywhere," Namo said angrily. "How can that be?"

Fargo admitted he was stumped. They were traveling north, the direction the creature went that night it paid them a near visit. It was also the direction the Mad Indian went. They stopped at every island, every hummock, every bump of land. They looked for tracks, scat, places where a large creature might have bedded down. They found nothing.

The only conclusion Fargo could come to, the only thing that made any sense, was that the so-called monster spent nearly all its time in the water. A lot of animals did—snakes, frogs, alligators—but they all came out on land. Only fish spent their entire time in water, and whatever the monster was, Fargo was sure of one thing—it damn sure wasn't a fish.

Fargo began to understand why the Cajuns who hunted the thing never found it. The beast was either incredibly intelligent or incredibly wary, or both. Its senses were superior to human senses, and it knew the swamp better than they did.

Then there was the Mad Indian.

Fargo didn't know what to make of him. That the Indian showed up after they heard the creature the other night suggested the Indian was following it. But why anyone, even a lunatic, would follow an animal that was going around attacking and killing people, was beyond him.

Namo had been excited the morning after they heard the thing. He was certain they would catch up to it before nightfall. But by the third day he was glum, and by the fourth morning he was scowling at the world and everything in it.

That evening they camped on a strip of land so deep in the swamp, it was doubtful any other white man ever set foot there. Clovis gathered wood and Namo kindled the fire. Fargo put coffee on.

The one bright spot was Halette. She talked, but only when spoken to. Not once, though, did Fargo see her smile. Most of the time she sat in the pirogue with her head bowed, a portrait of misery.

To complicate things, their provisions were running low. They could make do for another three or four days, provided they came across game to shoot.

All these factors combined led Fargo to remark, "We should head back to the settlement tomorrow."

"To Gros Ville?" Namo looked about to argue the point. But he sighed and said, "*Oui*. I suppose it is best. We will rest a few days, buy more supplies, and head out again."

"Without your kids."

"What?" Clovis said.

"We have been all through that," Namo reminded him. "You agreed they could come."

"Look at your daughter. Your son is wore out, too. Find someone to leave them with or you can come out again by yourself." Fargo tried to soften the sting by adding, "We can cover more area by ourselves, make better time."

Clovis objected. "No, Papa. Don't listen to him. I want to be with you. I loved Mama. I have that right."

"You will do as I say," Namo responded. "I don't want to leave you but the scout has a point. You do slow us down, if only a little."

From that moment on Clovis didn't hide his resentment. Where he had been friendly, he was now cold.

Fargo didn't care. He had been hired to do a job. The children were complications he could do without.

The next morning they headed back. That night they thought they heard, far off in the distance, the squeals and shrieks of the thing they hunted. But it didn't come near them.

They were a day out from the settlement when they rounded a cluster of cypress and came on a large island. Half a dozen pirogues had been drawn up, and as many tents and lean-tos erected. Several campfires were going. Hunters or trappers, he thought, until Namo Heuse stiffened.

"We will try to slip by without them seeing us."

"Why? What's wrong?"

"Listen to me. If they see us, let me do the talking. And if they want us to join them, keep your guns close and don't turn your back on anyone."

"Damn it, Namo. What's going on?"

Suddenly they were spotted. Someone shouted and armed men hurried to the water's edge. More were by the tents, along with three women. So they weren't hunters or trappers, after all.

A broad-shouldered Cajun wearing blue pants and a red sash with a pair of pistols tucked under it waved and smiled and called out to them in French. Then his gaze settled on Fargo and he switched to English. "Namo? That is you, isn't it? With your little ones? Come pay me a visit."

"*Oui*," Namo answered, and stroked for the island.

Fargo didn't like the looks some of them gave him. It wasn't outright hostility but it was close to it. "Who are they?"

Namo didn't answer.

Their pirogue glided in close and waiting hands pulled it onto dry land. The man in the red sash helped Halette out, saying gallantly, "It is a pleasure to see you again, princess. And you too, young Clovis."

Namo put his hands on their shoulders. "I didn't

expect to find you so near Gros Ville. The last I knew, you were camped well to the south of here."

The broad-shouldered man shrugged. "I must move around a lot. As you know, there are some who would love to put a knife into my back." He turned to Fargo. "But who have we here? A new friend, eh? Perhaps you would be so kind as to introduce me."

"Skye Fargo," Namo said, "permit me to introduce Remy Cuvier."

For once Fargo's poker face failed him. He shook, and was surprised by the other's strength.

"Ah. You have heard of me, I see. I trust the stories have been flattering?" Remy laughed. So did some of his men.

A sallow Cajun with a pockmarked face said, "We don't like outsiders. We don't like them at all."

"Now, now, Onfroi. He is with Namo and Namo is family and you will treat them as I do, yes?"

Onfroi nodded but he was not happy about it.

"Family?" Fargo said to Namo Heuse.

"I didn't tell you? Remy is my wife's cousin. Or was, I should say."

"*Oui.* I have spent many a happy night at their cabin," Remy declared, and patted Halette on the cheek. "When these little ones were infants, I bounced them on my knee. I love them dearly."

Fargo said, "You're not what I expected."

"You imagined an ogre, perhaps?" Remy was a great one for laughing. "After all, I am the terror of the swamp, am I not?"

"To hear everyone talk," Fargo replied.

"I am not a terror to my own kind, monsieur. I have never killed a fellow Cajun. Outsiders, yes. And there are some of my own kind who hold that against me." Remy paused. "They don't understand, as I do, that outsiders always bring trouble."

Namo said quickly, "I sent for him, Remy, to help me kill the monster that killed Emmeline. He is a famous plainsman."

"Who is far from his plain. But no matter. Emmeline is no longer with us but you are still family and under my protection. And those with you, as well." Remy gave his men a meaningful glance and put his hands on his pistols. "If there is anyone who thinks it should be otherwise, now is the time to say so."

No one did, although Onfroi shifted his weight from foot to foot and fingered the hilt of a stag-handled knife.

Remy escorted them to one of the fires and indicated logs they could sit on. He clapped his hands and demanded drink and food, and two women hustled over and filled tin cups with coffee for Fargo and Namo. Clovis and Halette were given tea.

As Fargo sipped he noticed that Remy's men had casually spread out and formed a ring around them.

"So tell me what you have been up to?" Remy prompted.

Namo related their hunt, and when he came to the part about hearing squeals and something big moving in the swamp, Remy interrupted him with, "We have heard it too. Several times. One night it came quite close. I ordered my men to throw wood on the fires and we stood with our rifles ready but the thing did not attack. I swear to you, though, that I saw its eyes off in the dark. They glowed as red as the pits of hell."

"Fargo is of the opinion it is afraid of fire," Namo mentioned.

"He could well be right. We always keep our fires going all night. Perhaps that is why it has left us alone."

"Have you seen the Mad Indian too?" Fargo asked.

"Him?" Remy laughed. He shifted on his log and crooked a finger at a man leaning against a tree. "Breed! Come over here, if you would."

Part Cajun and part Indian, the Breed wore Cajun clothes but had his hair in braids and a hawk feather tied to the braid on the left. His waist bristled with revolvers and knives and what Fargo at first mistook for a tomahawk but turned out to be a hatchet. "Yes, my friend?"

"This one"—Remy indicated Fargo—"wants to know about the Mad Indian."

"And you want me to enlighten him? Very well." The Breed hooked his thumbs in his belt. "The Mad Indian is the last of his people. His was a small tribe, the Quinipissa. Many years ago they fled into the swamp after a fight with La Salle, the Frenchman. Later a white trader gave them smallpox, and they all died save for the mad one. Now he hates whites, hates them so much, his hate has made him mad."

Fargo frowned. White diseases, it was said, had killed more Indians than all the white guns combined.

"How do you know all this?" Namo inquired.

"I have Washa blood. I hear things you wouldn't."

"But what has this Mad Indian to do with the creature that killed my wife?" Namo wondered.

"That I wouldn't know."

As Fargo listened, he became aware that one of the women was eyeing him as a hungry man might eye a side of beef. A shapely brunette whose wafer-thin dress clung tight, she had green eyes, high cheekbones, and inviting pink lips. When he glanced at her she boldly met his gaze, her hands on her hips, her pose saying all that need be said.

Nothing escaped Remy. He caught their looks, and chuckled. "Perhaps I should introduce Pensee. She has been with me for four years now, and there is no finer female anywhere."

"*Merci,*" Pensee said.

"Is she your woman?" Fargo asked.

Pensee answered for herself. "I belong to no man. Remy befriended me when no one else would. For that, he earned my friendship, and my loyalty."

"She had acquired—how shall I put this?" Remy said, with a flick of his eyes at Halette. "A certain reputation. The prim and proper wanted nothing to do with her, so I took her into my fold."

"Decent of you."

"Not at all," Remy candidly admitted. "My motive

was selfish. I have too few women in my merry band."

Fargo asked her, "Do you hate outsiders too?"

"To me a man is a man," Pensee said. "His race, his color, matter little. It is how he is under the sheets."

"What do you mean?" Halette asked.

Remy scowled at Pensee, then smiled and said to the girl, "She means she doesn't like men who snore in bed."

"*Mon père* snores."

"*C'est très ennuyeux*," Pensee said.

"*Ca m'est egal. Ne vous en faites pas.*"

"What a charming child."

"Enough," Remy warned. "She is a delight. You could learn from her if you weren't so full of yourself."

Pensee walked off, her hips threatening to rip loose from her spine.

"She has a temper, that one," Remy said, and chuckled.

Fargo had no desire to spend the night but he didn't see how he could get out of it short of fighting his way off the island. And there were simply too many for him to take on alone. Then, too, he had an obligation to Namo. To say nothing of his fondness for the girl.

As the evening wore on, the men relaxed and mingled. All save Onfroi, who hung in the background like a vulture circling a carcass. Fargo got a crick in his neck from keeping an eye on him.

Clovis and Halette liked Remy. That was plain to see. Halette sat on his leg and they listened to tales of his wild times. Tales toned down, Fargo suspected, so as not to shock them. It was obvious Remy cared for them as much as they did for him. So much for the hard-hearted scourge of the Atchafalaya Swamp.

Namo insisted his children turn in at ten. "They have had a long day and we have a long way to go tomorrow to reach Gros Ville."

"You are giving up the hunt?"

"Never! I won't rest until the thing that killed my Emmeline is a pile of rotting flesh."

Remy offered his tent to Namo and the children. As for Fargo, "You may sleep where you will. We can lend you blankets if you need them. But be warned. It's not uncommon for us to find snakes in them when we wake up in the morning. They like the warmth."

"I know about snakes," Fargo said. Rattlers did the same thing. "And we have our own blankets."

The spot Fargo chose was under a cypress a stone's throw from the southernmost fire. He bundled a blanket for a pillow and then spread out another and was about to lie down when a figure detached itself from the shadows. Instinctively, suspecting it was Onfroi, he swooped his hand to his Colt.

"Don't shoot me, monsieur," Pensee teased, coming over and standing so that her chest practically touched his.

"To what do I owe the pleasure?"

"If I have to tell you, then perhaps you don't know what pleasure is."

9

Fargo glanced toward the large tent and the silhouettes backlit from within by a lantern. "What about Remy?"

"What about him?" Pensee rejoined. "I'm free to do as I want. To be with who I want. And from the moment I laid eyes on you, I wanted you."

The camp lay quiet under the stars. About half the men had turned in. The rest were swapping stories at the fires or playing cards or rolling dice. None were paying the least bit of attention to Pensee.

"What's the matter? Can it be you are afraid? I didn't take you for timid." She snickered. "Or is it that you don't like women?"

"If I liked them any more, I'd own my own whorehouse."

"Is that so?" Pensee pressed her bosom to his chest, her hips to his hips. "Then why hesitate? Life is too short for hesitation. We must take what we want when we want or we may never get to take it at all."

"Is that your outlook on life?" Fargo was scanning the camp to be sure they weren't being watched. He didn't see Onfroi anywhere and that bothered him.

"It is the only one to have. Why deprive ourselves of the pleasures life offers? Of food and drink and, yes, intimacy." Pensee lightly ran a fingertip along Fargo's chin. "Me, I deprive myself nothing. This way, when I die, I won't have any regrets."

"None of these gents are going to try and stick a knife in me?"

"Are you always so cautious?" Pensee rose onto

the tips of her toes and nipped his chin with her teeth. "What if one did? *C'est la vie*, eh?"

"Doesn't that mean 'that's life'?"

"*Oui.*"

"You're not worth dying over."

Offended, Pensee took a step back and put her hands on her hips. "That's a fine thing to say to a lady who is offering herself to you. Have you no respect?"

"I could ask the same of you. You're the one who doesn't seem to care if I get stabbed or shot for touching you."

Pensee burst into peals of mirth. "Touché. I admit I am thinking of only one thing." She stepped up close again and placed her hand on his manhood. "I am thinking of this."

Fargo felt himself stir. "Damn, you are a tease."

"And you like it, admit it?" Pensee ran her hand over his hardening pole. "Goodness. You grow and grow."

A constriction had formed in Fargo's throat and he had to cough before he could say, "Isn't there somewhere private?"

"Are you shy?" Pensee asked, and tittered. "Men! They act so big and tough. But in a woman's hand they are kittens."

"I'll give you kittens," Fargo said, and plunged his hand between her thighs. At the contact she arched her back and her mouth parted in a tremulous gasp.

"Oh! No."

"What's the matter? Are you shy?" Fargo gave as good as he got.

Pensee glanced toward the other fires and the tents, then clasped his hand and pulled him around the cypress to the other side. "One thing I am not is that, monsieur," she said huskily. "But like you I don't need an audience. That is how I got into trouble before I met Remy."

"Trouble how?"

"There was this gentleman who shared my lack of inhibitions. We let people watch for money. You would think the world was coming to an end, to hear the upstanding citizens who wanted us hung for our crime."

"There are limits," Fargo said. Not that he had room to talk. He had done more than a few things in his time that most would brand scandalous.

"Not for me. Not then. Not now. Not ever. I like to live to the fullest. And if some are upset, that is their nature, not mine."

"Did you bring me behind this tree to make love or talk me to death?" Fargo asked.

"Talk is a poor second to making love."

With that Pensee melted into his arms. Her molten mouth fastened to his and her lips widened to admit his tongue. She groaned when he sucked on hers. He cupped a breast, pinched the nipple.

The night was suddenly a lot warmer.

Fargo pressed her against the tree. Her arms rose to hook around his neck and her pelvis glued itself to his. It occurred to him that he had left the Henry lying on his blanket but he decided to leave it there. He doubted anyone would be stupid enough to try and steal it.

"Why did you stop? Don't you know what to do next?"

"I reckon I do." Fargo rubbed his forefinger across her nether lips; she wasn't wearing undergarments. She shivered and cooed and bit his shoulder, and not lightly, either.

"Do that again."

Fargo did, dipping the tip of his finger into her. She ground against him and lathered his neck and his ear. At the same time she pried at his buckskin shirt, raising it so she could slide her hands underneath and rove them over his muscular chest and knotted belly.

"Nice. Very nice."

Fargo could say the same but chatter was a distraction he could do without. He shut her up with another kiss and kept his lips there while he kneaded and tweaked her breasts. Soon her chest was heaving. Her breath fanned his throat as she bent to run her tongue from one side to the other.

By now Fargo's pants bulged. He needed release. Unbuckling his belt, he lowered his holster and the Colt, then let his pants slide down around his knees. As his pole came free she let out a soft cry of delight.

"*Mon Dieu!* I have struck gold."

Eagerly, she enfolded him with her fingers. Fargo had to clamp down a mental lid to keep from exploding before he was ready. The constriction returned as she delicately ran her fingernails up and down and then cupped his jewels.

"I would like to chop this off and keep it with me always."

Fargo's rising ardor deflated. He looked at her, half inclined to swat her hands away. "What did you just say?"

"I was joking. I wouldn't cut you, my handsome tug-mutton. It is just that you are a stallion."

"Your handsome what?"

Pensee didn't reply. She had tucked at the knees, and the next Fargo felt, his member was sheathed in velvet. He braced an arm against the tree and closed his eyes.

The velvet sensation went away but only long enough for Pensee to ask, "You like, yes?"

"I like, yes," Fargo confirmed, and gave himself up to the pleasure. She stayed tucked a good long while. Several times she brought him close to the brink but each time she showed the savvy not to send him over.

"Damn, you're good."

"*Merci.* But in truth I am bad." And Pensee chortled in naughty glee.

Fargo pulled her to her feet, spread her legs, inserted his tip, and looked into her eager eyes. "Ready?"

"Always."

A lunge, and Fargo rammed up into her. For a few seconds she was still, transfixed with rapture. Then her body began to move of its own accord and Fargo went with the flow, ramming ever harder and steadily faster until she tossed her head wildly and thrashed uncontrollably. But she didn't cry out. Instead, she sank her teeth into his shoulder.

Fargo didn't stop. Her velvet sheath grew wetter. At his next thrust she went into a paroxysm of ecstasy, lost in the delirium of another release. Fargo kept ramming. She clung to him, spent but wanting more. He rocked on his boots, virtually lifting her off the ground. Then his own moment came, and it was everything it always was, the moment when a man felt most alive, the moment a man lived for.

Covered with sweat, they coasted to a stop and Pensee sagged and whispered, "*Étonnant.*"

"Eh?"

"It was wonderful. I thank you."

"Any time."

"I will hold you to that." Pensee kissed him, then closed her eyes. "I am so tired and content I could fall asleep standing up."

"No need for that." Fargo slid out of her and pulled himself together. As he strapped on his Colt he heard splashing from the swamp. Not much, and not loud. A gator, he figured.

They walked around the cypress to his blanket. The Henry was where it should be.

Fargo sat and patted a spot next to him. "You're welcome to join me if you want."

"I would like nothing better. But I usually sleep by myself so as not to have the men jealous of one another. *Comprendre vous?*"

Fargo shrugged and sank onto his back. "Whatever you think best."

"Tomorrow is another day, yes?"

Struggling to stay awake, Fargo rose onto his elbows and stared after her until she went into a tent. Then sleep claimed him and he knew nothing until his eyes snapped open and he lay there wondering what woke him.

Fargo felt sluggish, as if his blood was pumping in slow motion. He was content to lie there and drift back to sleep. He closed his eyes and rolled onto his side, and that was when the strangeness struck him.

There wasn't a sound to be heard.

The swamp had gone completely still. A silence so deep, not even a mosquito buzzed. No croaks, no bellows, no roars, no screeches, no bleats of any kind.

Puzzled, Fargo raised his head. He couldn't see many of the stars through the canopy but he did spy the Big Dipper and by its position he guessed it had to be close to four in the morning. He slowly sat up.

The fires had gone out and the tents were dark. Fargo remembered Remy saying that they never let the fires die at night. He wondered if whoever was keeping watch had fallen asleep. He debated getting up but decided he was worrying over nothing and was about to lie back down when a darkling silhouette appeared, moving toward the water, with an odd hopping gait.

What the hell? Fargo thought. There was something familiar about the figure but he didn't realize what until a low titter reached his ears. Grabbing the Henry, he rose. The figure had reached a canoe and was clambering in. Fargo ran toward it as a paddle swished. The canoe faded into the dark.

Fargo came to the water, and stopped.

From out of the night came another titter. And something else. "Mad, mad, mad, mad, mad!"

"Hell." Fargo turned and raced toward the tents. Smoke was rising from the nearest fire so it hadn't been out long. He stopped and hunkered to poke at the charred logs and get the fire going again but someone had poured water on it. Three guesses who.

Fargo moved to the next fire. It, too, had been doused with water. And sprawled beside it on his stomach was the man on guard. Bending, Fargo saw that the back of the man's head had been caved in by a heavy blow. He rolled the body over and Onfroi's empty eyes stared up at him.

The Mad Indian's handiwork.

Fargo imagined how it had been. Onfroi, perhaps

dozing by the fire, the insane old warrior creeping up the shore and striking him from behind with the hatchet or a rock and then dousing the fires and fleeing. But why put out the fires? Fargo wondered. Why not use the fire as a weapon and set the tents ablaze? Maybe kill a few more hated whites?

Suddenly a low, rumbling grunt issued from the trees beyond the tents.

Ice filled Fargo's veins. Now he knew why the Mad Indian had doused the fires. He turned to shout a warning but he had figured it out too late.

Out of the night it hurtled, a living engine of destruction. As big as the biggest grizzly, as powerful as a bull buffalo, it emitted a strident squeal of fury and tore into a tent. Canvas ripped and tent poles snapped, and then men were screaming and cursing and the thing came ripping out the other side with part of the tent clinging to its bulk and a limp human form flapping up and down in front of it. The creature tossed the body aside, wheeled with lightning swiftness, and charged a second tent.

Fargo jerked the Henry to his shoulder and snapped off a shot. If he scored the slug had no effect. In the blink of an eye the second tent was reduced to ruin and there were more screams and curses added to the din.

The monster was wreaking havoc.

Fargo ran toward it, thinking that if he got closer he could try for a head shot. The tent exploded and out it came, bearing down on him. He fixed a hasty bead but before he could fire he was slammed aside as if he were a twig. A pale, curved . . . something . . . flashed before his face, missing by a whisker. He hit hard on his back, the breath knocked out of him.

Bedlam reigned.

Men were swearing, shouting, voicing their death wails. Guns boomed. Women shrieked. Above it all rose the squeals and screeches of the beast as it ran amok, destroying and slaying in a wanton rage. The thing was unstoppable. Fargo saw a man run up and fire a revolver, the muzzle inches from the creature's head, but it had no more effect than his own shot.

The creature's head swept up and the man sailed end over end, catapulted through the air as effortlessly as Fargo might toss a pebble. The man thudded to the ground only an arm's-length away and wet drops spattered Fargo's face and neck. He half rose, his gorge rising too at the sight of the Cajun's ruptured belly and chest. The creature had ripped the man open from navel to neck, tearing through clothes and flesh and bone, and the man's organs were spilling out.

Fargo groped for the Henry and found it.

More men were down. There were scattered bodies everywhere.

And then the voice of the woman Fargo had made love to just hours ago wailed in desperate terror, "Help me! Someone please help me!"

Fargo rose and raced to Pensee's rescue.

10

Her cry came from a tent that was still standing.

Fargo ran toward it. Without warning the side burst outward and the beast, squealing ferociously, was on him. Fargo dived to one side. He glimpsed it as it went by, glimpsed the gleam of a curved tusk and a hide covered with bristly hair. Its hooves drummed past his ear.

Another second, and something struck Fargo across the shoulders, something heavy. Dazed by the blow, for a few harrowing seconds he thought the creature had turned on him.

Then someone groaned.

Fargo rolled and pushed. The person on top of him slid off, and he rose to his knees. He still had the Henry and he jammed it to his shoulder.

The creature was streaking toward a lean-to. In it huddled two men too terrified to do more than scream as the beast smashed into their flimsy sanctuary and reduced it, and them, to crushed ruins.

Fargo fired. He was sure he hit it but the thing didn't break stride or stop. It crashed off into the night, the brush and the trees no hindrance at all.

Figuring it was circling to come at them again, Fargo waited. He was going to empty the Henry into it, if that was what it took to bring it down. But the crashing faded and the creature didn't reappear. He became conscious of moans and sobs from all around him, and he glanced down at the person who had been thrown on top of him.

"Oh, hell."

Pensee had been ripped open just like Onfroi. Only in her case, a tusk had penetrated just above the junction of her legs and ripped in a zigzag pattern clear up to the base of her throat. Thankfully, her eyes were closed. One breast, untouched, was exposed. Her dress was shredded; he pulled part of it up to cover her.

Only then did Fargo think of the Heuses. Whirling, he ran to where the biggest tent lay in shattered tatters. "Halette! Namo! Clovis!"

"Under here!"

Fargo kicked a broken pole aside and hauled at the flattened canvas. Underneath, covering his son and daughter with his body, was Namo.

"Is it safe?"

"The thing is gone." Fargo pulled the canvas out of the way and offered his hand to help them stand. "Any of you hurt?"

"*Non*, thank God." Namo brushed dirt from Halette. "I woke up and got them down on the ground barely in time."

"Where's Remy?" Fargo asked, looking all around.

"He was in a cot on the other side."

Fargo moved another piece of canvas. He found the broken cot, and a prone, still Remy. Quickly kneeling, Fargo rolled him over. He expected to find Remy had been gored like the others but the only wound was a gash on the temple. A tusk or a hoof had struck him a glancing blow. Slipping his hand under Remy's shoulder, he dragged him clear of the debris and held him propped against his leg.

The Breed ran up, pale and limping. "Is he dead? Tell me that *bête* hasn't killed him too?"

"Fetch some water."

"*Oui*. Right away."

Halette came up and stood at Fargo's elbow. "Is Uncle Remy dead? Has the monster killed him like it did my *mère*?"

"Your uncle will live," Fargo assured her. "And it's

no monster." He knew what it was now. One of the most vicious, and crafty, of all the animals there were anywhere.

Namo had come up. "If you know what that fiend is, don't keep it to yourself."

Remy groaned, then blinked, and looked about him in confusion. "What? Where?"

"Stay still," Fargo advised. "You were hit on the head and you're bleeding pretty bad. You need a bandage."

But Remy didn't lie still. He twisted, stared in horror at the carnage, then sat bolt upright. He put a hand to the gash, stared at the wet blood on his fingertips, and rose. "It can't be. That brute did all this!"

It was then the Breed returned bearing a tin cup filled with water. He held it out to Remy but Remy angrily swatted it aside. "How many?" he demanded, and grabbed the Breed by the front of his shirt. "How many, damn you?"

"I haven't checked."

Remy shoved him. "Do it! Now!" He took a step but his legs wobbled and he started to pitch forward. Namo caught him and held him, and Halette clasped his hand.

"Are you all right, Uncle Remy?"

"*Oui*, child," Remy said as Namo lowered him so he could sit.

Fargo was listening to the sounds of the swamp. The frogs were croaking again, the crickets chirping, the gators bellowing. The beast was gone. Or was it? It might be lurking out there, watching and girding to finish what it had started.

"Did any of you see the thing?" Remy asked Namo and his children. "Do you know what it is?"

"He does," Namo said, nodding at Fargo.

"What could possibly do all this?" Remy swept an arm at the bodies and the shattered tents. "The cries it made. It didn't sound like a bear."

"It wasn't."

"Well? Tell us, damn you."

"The monster of the Atchafalaya Swamp is a razorback."

"What was that you said?"

"A razorback. A wild boar."

Remy uttered a sharp bark of disbelief. "You're crazy. I caught a glimpse of it as it came through our tent. It was gigantic. Bigger than the biggest black bear." He shook his head, and winced. "No. Hogs don't grow that size. They just don't."

"Some razorbacks do."

Fargo recalled hearing somewhere that the first hogs were brought to America long ago by the Spaniards. Some escaped and reverted to the wild. They multiplied like rabbits. Now, razorbacks were common from Texas to the Carolinas. A normal boar grew to no more than four or five hundred pounds but every now and then a giant one appeared, twice that size, a king among its kind, a thousand pounds of might and malice with tusks a foot long and a hide so thick that most slugs barely penetrated.

"*Mon Dieu*," Namo breathed. "To think! My fair Emmeline was killed by a *pig*."

"A razorback out to kill everyone it comes across," Fargo amended. He also recalled that boars were known to roam territories of fifty square miles or more.

"Our fires should have kept it away," Remy said. "My men knew better than to let them go out."

Fargo told him about the Mad Indian, and the dousing.

"Wait. Are you saying the Mad Indian is *helping* the thing? That the Mad Indian put out our fires just so this boar would attack us?"

"That's ridiculous," Namo said.

"Is it?" Fargo countered. "The Mad Indian hates whites. He blames us for the smallpox that wiped out his people. He follows the razorback and does what he can to help it kill as many of us as it can."

"Can it truly be?"

"The razorback would kill the Mad Indian, too, wouldn't it?" Clovis asked them.

"Not if he was careful."

Out of the dark came the Breed. His shoulders were slumped and he tried twice to say, "Only three."

"Only three what?" Remy said.

"Besides you and me, only three of us are still alive and they won't last long."

As if to accent the point, sobs were borne by the breeze.

Remy grabbed the Breed by the shoulders. "The women! Not the women too? Where is Pensee? And Delmare?"

"I—" the Breed began, and sadly shook his head. "I am sorry, my friend. All the women are dead. Pensee is one of the worst. The beast split her like a melon."

"No!" Remy looked wildly about. "*All* of them? All our friends? All those we called brothers and sisters?"

"All."

Halette began crying.

Remy sank to his knees and wrapped his arms around himself. Chin bowed, he said morosely, "They counted on me. I was their leader. I was to keep them safe."

"You took precautions," the Breed said. "No one could have foreseen this."

"I should have," Remy insisted. "A good leader thinks of everything. I should have had two men on guard, not just one."

"You're being too hard on yourself."

Fargo agreed. There was no way in hell anyone could have guessed a giant razorback was running amok in the Atchafalaya.

"This razorback has never done anything like this before," the Breed was saying. "It has never attacked so many people at once."

Another good point, and food for Fargo's thought. Until now, except for Emmeline and Halette, the thing attacked only those who were alone.

"Show me the women," Remy said, rising. "Show me each of them."

"You don't need to see."

"Yes, I do. I want it seared into my memory so I never forget." Remy motioned and the Breed led the way.

Halette held out her arms to Namo and he squatted and hugged her. "There, there, little one. God was watching over us. None of us were harmed."

"But those nice ladies. I want to go home, Papa. I want to sleep in my own bed. I want our roof over my head." Halette stared wide-eyed out over the great swamp. "I don't want to be here any more."

"We will leave in the morning."

"Please. Now. I'm afraid."

Fargo turned and walked to the water's edge. He thought of Pensee, of her ravaged body. He thought of how close the razorback came to killing him. And then and there he decided he wasn't leaving Louisiana until the creature was dead. "No matter how long it takes," he said out loud.

"How long what takes?"

Fargo nearly jumped. "Damn, boy. Don't sneak up on folks like that."

Clovis was glumly cradling his rifle. "*Pardon.* I couldn't bear to watch my sister weep."

"Me either."

"This razorback. How can it be so big and yet be so fast? It was faster than any horse. Faster even than deer."

"I wouldn't go that far." But Fargo agreed it was ungodly quick. Anyone who tried to outrun it wouldn't have a prayer.

"I used to love the swamp," Clovis said. "It has been my home since I was born. I know the animals, the birds, the trails. The gators and the snakes, they don't scare me like they scare some. But this—" and the boy gestured at the inky veil. "I want no part of this. I have lost my mama. I would not lose my papa or my sister as well."

"Let's hope it doesn't come to that."

"Help me, Monsieur Fargo. Talk to him. Talk to my father and convince him to give up the hunt. Now, while he still can. Before it's too late."

"I doubt he'd listen to me. You should talk to him yourself. Blood counts for more than the advice of a stranger."

"You mean the blood in our veins?" Clovis said. "Yes, I'm his son, but I'm only a boy. You are a grown man."

"You talk old for your age. Give it a try. What can it hurt?"

Along the shore came the Breed. He didn't say anything. He stopped and did as they were doing: stared out over the sinister swamp.

"Where is Uncle Remy?" Clovis asked.

"With your father." The Breed poked a clump of grass with his toe. "They are going to join forces. For Remy this is personal now. He won't rest until he has his revenge."

"What about you?"

"Where Remy goes, I am, always," the Breed said. "We are brothers, him and I. Not in body but inside." He thumped his chest with a fist.

Fargo asked, "Do you have a name?" Few men liked being called breeds. To many it was an insult.

A look of surprise came over him. "Yes. I am called Hetsutu. In your tongue that would be Yellow Jacket." He smiled. "You are the second white man to ever ask."

"Who was the first?"

"Remy Cuvier."

Wind gusted from the swamp, bringing with it a far distant squeal and then the shriek of a hapless animal caught in the razorback's rampaging path.

"It doesn't kill just people," Clovis said.

"No," Hetsutu replied. "The madness is in its veins. It kills everything, and it won't stop killing until it is dead. Many more lives will be lost if we do not stop it."

"White lives," Fargo said.

"You suggest it isn't my fight? But Remy is white and he is my friend. Pensee was a good friend, too. Even Onfroi treated me as an equal." Hetsutu squared his shoulders. "I have told you I am part Washa. Perhaps the last of my kind. I swear to you on the blood of my ancestors that I am with you in this. Come what may."

"Come what may," Fargo said.

The wind off the swamp suddenly seemed chill.

11

The two pirogues glided along the bayou in the bright of day.

Fargo was in the second craft with Namo and the kids. Remy and Hetsutu were up ahead.

"We will reach Gros Ville by nightfall," Namo announced. He did not sound happy about it.

"It's for the best."

They had talked it over, all of them, and agreed that the smart thing to do, the safe thing to do, was take the children to the settlement and leave them with someone Namo trusted. Then the men would begin the hunt for the razorback.

But Namo had balked. He insisted on keeping his children at his side. It took a lot of arguing to get him to change his mind. Remy finally did it by saying that if Namo really loved them, he wouldn't expose them to the danger of what Remy called "that vile horror."

"No one can say I don't love my children," Namo had bristled.

"Then prove it."

Now here they were.

They had agreed to spend a couple of days in Gros Ville resting. Fargo and Namo needed it. Namo, especially. They were worn down and on edge from living in constant peril.

"But what about Remy?" Namo had brought up. "Some of the people there see him only as a criminal."

Remy had laughed that big laugh of his. "What do I care about those sheep? They will do nothing. Oh, they'll talk behind my back, and say how terrible I am, and how I should be punished, but they won't raise a hand against me." He had clapped Namo on the back. "Don't worry about me. I have friends who will put me up."

"But if you are seen?"

"I will keep to myself. Trust me. I will not let anything or anyone keep me from having my vengeance. I swear before God that I won't rest until that boar is dead."

That was their common bond. The shared conviction that the rogue razorback must be slain.

They debated asking their fellow Cajuns for help.

"We can organize hunting parties," Namo proposed. "Have twenty or thirty men sweep the swamp."

"And maybe drive it so far back in that it won't come back out for weeks," Remy said. "No, it's better if we keep the hunting party small. Just the four of us are enough."

"I agree," Hetsutu sided with him.

The whole way, Fargo was bothered by the feeling that they were being followed. Countless times he glanced over his shoulder but he never saw anything to account for it. He doubted it was the razorback. The boar made too much noise. But then again, when a wild boar wanted to, it could move with the stealth of a cougar.

For a while Fargo thought it might be the Mad Indian, but not once did Fargo spot him. He decided the lunatic wouldn't risk venturing so near the settlement.

Just nerves, Fargo figured.

Now, with sunlight playing over their pirogue, Halette remarked, "I can't wait to sleep in a bed again."

"I don't want to stay in Gros Ville," Clovis said to his father. "I want to be with you."

"What have I told you, son? You will stay with your sister and that is that." Namo stopped paddling to turn and put a hand on the boy's shoulder. "With your mother gone, we must look after one another. Can I count on you to watch over Halette while I am away?"

"*Oui*, Papa."

"And if I don't come back—"

"Don't say that."

"Don't ever talk like that," Halette echoed.

"Very well. But remember. Always be there for one another. You are brother and sister. That is a special bond. Never let anyone break you apart."

Fargo stroked his paddle and watched out for gators and snakes. He'd seen a coral snake the day before, and Namo mentioned that of all the snakes in Louisiana, coral snakes had the most potent venom.

"One bite and you will have fire in your veins and die."

Fargo was changing his mind about the swamp. The dangers outweighed the splendor. He had to admire the people who lived there. They possessed uncommon courage.

He couldn't wait to get back to his familiar prairies and mountains. They had their perils too, but they were nothing like this.

From the first pirogue came a shout. Remy was pointing.

Up ahead, finally, was Gros Ville. Other pirogues and canoes lined the landing. Only a few people were out and about in the heat of the day and no one paid much attention to them as they tied off.

They came to a side street and Remy stopped.

"Down here is where my friends live. We will separate and meet back at the landing three days from now, at sunrise."

Namo was carrying Halette. "I have a friend. Hopefully he and his woman will agree to put my children up."

That left Fargo on his own. He bent his steps to the tavern. It was early yet, and only a few customers were drinking and playing cards. He made straight for the bar.

Liana looked up from a ledger she was scribbling in. She gave a start and put a hand to her throat. "Are my eyes deceiving me?"

"Enough of your antics. Give me a bottle of your

best." Fargo fished in his pocket and slapped down a coin.

"I'm delighted you are back."

"The bottle, wench."

"*Certainement*. Here. I have missed you so much, it's on the house."

Fargo gratefully chugged. The whiskey burned his mouth and throat and exploded once it reached his empty stomach. He downed half the bottle in big gulps, thumped the bottle on the counter, and smacked his lips in satisfaction. "Damn, I needed that."

Liana touched his chin. "You look as if you haven't slept in days. And you haven't been eating well."

"The swamp will do that." Suddenly his weariness caught up with him, and Fargo leaned on the counter. "But I have three days to rest before we head out again."

"Three whole days?" Liana said with a playful grin, and promptly sobered. "Wait. Did I hear right? You're going out after that monster a second time?"

"Quit calling it that." Fargo explained, briefly, about his clashes with the terror of the Atchafalaya.

"A razorback?" Liana marveled. "Who would have thought it. But I don't like the idea of you out in the swamp."

"Makes two of us. But I'm being paid. And it's also become personal." Fargo didn't elaborate. He took the bottle and headed for the corner table, saying, "If you have the time and want to fix me a meal, I won't complain."

Liana laughed. "Would venison steak and potatoes and carrots do? A hunter traded me the meat for some rum."

Fargo's mouth watered. "That would do me fine."

"And coffee to wash it down?"

"I'll stick with the red-eye," Fargo said, patting the whiskey bottle. He wearily sank into a chair facing the door and propped his boots on the table. He figured to sit there the rest of the day. And if he was lucky, he might get to enjoy another bout under the sheets with Liana.

It took half an hour. The venison was juicy and delicious, the potatoes were seasoned and drowned in butter, and the carrots had a crunch to them. Liana also prepared a side of crayfish and a bowl of gumbo.

Fargo was ravenous. He relished every morsel. Intent on his food, he didn't pay much attention when two men hurried in and over to a nearby table where two others already sat. Their excited whispers were of no interest to him until he caught the word "Remy." He perked his ears.

"All I am saying is that we might never have a chance like this again."

"But to take the law into our own hands?"

"Whose law? Outsider law? What has that to do with us? We always take care of our own problems."

The last man fidgeted in his chair. "But that is just it, *mon ami*. Who says Remy is a problem?"

"He has killed," the stoutest of them said.

"Outsiders, yes. But never one of us. Never one of his own. Oh, I admit he is a scoundrel. Many accuse him of being a thief but I have yet to hear where he has stolen from any of us. Many say he is a bit of a bully but I have yet to hear of him bullying a fellow Cajun."

"All this is true," another said with a bob of his head.

"You make him out to be a saint," the stout man complained, "when he is a murderer."

"I make him out to be nothing but what he is. A rogue, yes. A hater of those who would impose their will on us, yes. A man of violence, yes. But I repeat. With his own kind he has always been as much a gentleman as anyone."

"I can't believe what my ears are hearing."

"Look, do as you want, Philippe. If you want to get men together and take him into custody, be our guest. But what then? Will you hand him over to the sheriff? Hand over one of your own kind?"

"To hear you, one would think all Cajuns were blood brothers."

"Aren't we?"

That ended their argument.

Fargo went on eating. He cracked open a crayfish and sucked out the sweet meat. He finished the gumbo. He forked the last piece of potato and was about to pop it into his mouth when the door opened and in came a young Cajun of twenty or so, his cap gone, his hair a mess, his clothes caked with mud, his pants torn. He lurched toward the bar, moving stiffly, a hand outstretched.

"Drink, Liana! In God's name give me a drink."

"Claude? What on earth?"

The other men came out of their chairs and hurried over to hear what the newcomer had to say.

Fargo stayed where he was; he could hear perfectly fine.

"A drink! A drink I say!" Claude clutched at the bottle Liana handed him and sucked greedily, his throat bobbing. "*Merci,*" he gasped, whiskey dribbling down his chin. "I needed that."

"Tell us what has you in this state," Liana coaxed. "Did you have an accident?"

"I'll say I did!" Claude declared. "And my accident has a name. Look at me!" He swept his hand at himself. "I am a mess. All thanks to the Mad Indian."

Fargo froze.

"The Mad Indian, you say?" the stout Cajun said. "Surely you don't mean he is somewhere near?"

"That is exactly what I mean," Claude confirmed. "Listen, my friends." He slumped against the bar. "I was on my way in from my cabin. My once-a-month visit for supplies. I wasn't more than half a mile from this very spot when I came around a cypress and there he was, sitting in his canoe, his back to me and staring this way."

"*Non!*"

"Yes, I tell you. I didn't know who he was at first. I took him for just another Indian. But as I came up next to him he heard me and he turned." Claude shuddered. "I tell you, as long as I live I will never

85

forget the look in his eyes. You can *see* the insanity. If I had any doubts they fled when he laughed and flapped his arms and said in English and French the same word over and over again."

"What word?" a man breathlessly asked.

"Mad," Claude said. "He kept saying, 'Mad, mad, mad, mad, mad!' "

"Dear God."

"To think he would dare come this close!"

Claude went on. "He laughed and then he brayed like a hound that has drank tainted water."

His audience was enrapt. So was Fargo. As he had learned the hard way, wherever you found the Mad Indian, you could be sure the razorback wasn't far off.

"What happened then, Claude? Did he try to kill you?"

"No. That is the strangest part."

"Strange how?"

"The Mad Indian just paddled away, looking at me over his shoulder and laughing."

"You didn't go after him?"

"I was too overcome with surprise. When I thought of it he was almost out of sight. He pointed this way, toward Gros Ville, and he shouted in poor French. Then English."

"What did he say?"

Claude swallowed more whiskey, then said, "He shouted that we are all going to die."

"Lunacy," a man said. "He is one and we are many."

"If he shows his face here, it will be his finish."

"Doesn't he realize what we will do to him?"

"Who can say? He's crazy. But one thing is certain. We need have no fear of the likes of him."

"No fear at all," another agreed.

All of them laughed or chuckled.

Not Fargo. He was thinking of Remy's camp and the ruptured bodies. And his skin crawled.

12

Night claimed the Atchafalaya.

Fargo stood under the stars out behind the tavern, patting the Ovaro and listening. He strained his ears for the sound he dreaded to hear but the usual chorus wasn't broken by the squeals of the razorback.

Fargo kept telling himself his worry was pointless. The settlement was too big. Nearly twenty buildings, and there had to be forty to fifty people, if not more, considering how many were at the tavern. What with the lights and the noise and the voices, the idea of the razorback attacking Gros Ville was silly. But then what was the Mad Indian doing there? Had the Mad Indian followed them out of the swamp? Was that why he thought they were being watched?

"I reckon I'm making too much of things," Fargo said to the Ovaro.

The door opened, spilling a rectangle of light, and out came Liana. She was wearing an apron over her dress and holding a cloth. "Here you are. Another couple of hours and I can close for the night."

"Have something in mind, do you?"

"I thought perhaps you and I could take up where • we left off." Liana grinned and swayed her hips. "That is, if you're not too tired to give me a back rub."

"I'll give you more than that."

Laughing merrily, she turned to go back in. "Oh. I thought you should know. There has been more talk of Remy. But they are going to leave him be."

"Any word from Namo?"

"No. He's staying with a friend in a shack at the

west end of the street. From what I am told, his children are happy to be out of the swamp. It is said that they went through a terrible ordeal out there." She looked at him. "You didn't tell me everything."

"I told you we tangled with the boar."

"You didn't tell me how many it killed." Liana shook her head in sorrow. "It *is* a monster, whether you think so or not. Word will spread quickly. I would imagine that by this time tomorrow, everyone for fifty miles around will have heard."

Fargo heard a distant splash. "Liana—"

"What?"

"Nothing. Just don't go anywhere tonight unless I'm with you."

"Where would I go? I have a business to run." Liana chuckled. "Have you grown so fond of me that you want me always near?"

"That must be it."

"Why don't I believe you? Very well. Don't say. But I promise not to leave unless I let you know."

"Good."

Liana reached for the door, then turned back to him. "What is it that concerns you so?"

"Where you find the Mad Indian, you find the razorback."

"Surely you are not suggesting what I think you are suggesting?"

"I'm just saying, is all."

"No." Liana stared into the dark and shook her head. "The beast would have to be as crazy as the Indian. There are too many of us."

"I think so too but you never know. Maybe you should spread the word. Warn them. But do it in a way they won't think you're loco."

"Dear God, I pray you are mistaken. Now I won't sleep a wink all night."

"That's all right. I was planning on keeping you up anyway."

"I can hardly wait."

The door closed on her laugh and Fargo was left to

ponder the swamp and the night. In his mind's eye he relived his glimpse of the razorback and tried to calculate how big it really was. Six feet high at the front shoulders, he guessed, and ten to twelve feet long. Foot-long tusks. Easily a thousand pounds. Maybe Liana was right—it *was* a monster.

The next consideration was how to kill it. Fargo had seen with his own eyes that its hide was proof against bullets. His Henry had proven useless. Clovis's Sharps might be powerful enough to bring it down but the shot must core its brain or its vitals and the boar wasn't about to stand still long enough for anyone to take sure aim.

Fargo shrugged and went in. Maybe he would ask to borrow the Sharps before they headed out.

The tavern was packed. The topic on everyone's tongue was the razorback. An old Cajun with a salt-and-pepper beard was saying to an attentive audience, "All of you know me. Like many of you, I've lived in this swamp all my life, and I say here and now that this animal can't be as big as they say."

"Namo claims different," someone said.

"Fear makes things seem bigger than they are."

"Are you calling Namo a coward?"

"No, no. But you've heard the story. Their fires were out. The thing was on them so fast, they didn't get a good look. Now I ask you. Is it unreasonable to suggest they have exaggerated without meaning to? I bet the razorback is no bigger than any other."

Fargo put an elbow on the bar. "You'd lose that bet, mister. I was there."

All eyes swung toward him. Few were outright friendly.

"You're the scout that's taken up with Liana?"

At the other end of the bar, Liana hollered, "Hear now. Watch what you say about me, Parfait, or you can go clear to New Orleans for your liquor from now on."

"I meant no offense, *chéri*," the old Cajun said. "You should know better." To Fargo he said, "I'm sorry but I just don't believe it. Why, someone told me the thing is as big as one of our shacks."

"If it was standing broadside in front of you, you couldn't see over it," Fargo told him.

"Hogwash." The old man realized what he had said, and he and several others laughed.

"Suit yourselves."

Fargo wasn't about to make a fool of himself trying to convince them. He went to his table and the cards. Now and again he caught snatches of talk. He half hoped Remy or Namo would show up, and when all the chatter abruptly ceased, he thought one of them had. But he was in for a surprise.

"Mind if I join you?" Hetsutu asked.

Fargo pushed out a chair with his foot. "Everyone is staring."

"Let them. As if I care what they think. They are bigots, many of them, and despise me for the part of me that is Indian."

"I've been meaning to ask you about that," Fargo said. "When I asked for your name, you told me your Indian name."

"So?"

"So you're part Cajun."

Hetsutu cracked a smile. "Half and half. That's me. And yes, I have a Cajun name but I never use it."

"So they're not the only bigots."

"No, they're not, and I am the first to admit it. Blame how I was treated when I was a boy. The half-breed, they called me. Or simply the Breed. As young as I was, I wasn't stupid. I saw how they looked down their noses at me. Parents wouldn't let their children play with me. And when my mother forced me to go to school for a year, the teacher made me sit by myself."

"It's rough being half and half." Fargo had seen plenty of race hate on the frontier. Whites who hated Indians because they were red; Indians who hated whites because they weren't red. Whites who hated blacks and blacks who hated whites and both hating the brown. One thing the world was never short on was hate.

"Don't take me wrong. I don't cry in my cups over it. I was born as I was born. But I don't have to like it, or like those who look at me as if I'm scum."

Fargo pushed his bottle across the table. "Have a drink, why don't you?"

"Is this your way of shutting me up?" Hetsutu grinned, and drank, and scowled. "It tastes as terrible as ever. No wonder I never acquired a taste for firewater."

"Are you out taking a stroll?"

Hetsutu peered at him over the bottle. "You're a sharp one. No. I came to talk to you. I've heard that the Mad Indian was spotted."

"It's all over Gros Ville by now."

"Do you know what that means? On my way over, I listened. The swamp is very still tonight. Too still."

"We share the same notion. But the good people of Gros Ville don't. They say there is no way in hell the razorback will attack here." Fargo accepted the bottle. "Whatever happens now is on their shoulders. I've done all I can."

"But have you really?"

"How's that?"

"Done all you can? I was thinking that you and I should get our rifles and keep watch. If we're right, we can shout to warn them."

"I was wrong about you," Fargo said. "A bigot wouldn't do what you want to do."

"Make no mistake. I couldn't care less about the men. But there are women and children. And I remember what that thing did to Pensce. She was my friend."

"I remember."

"Then you'll do it? Remy offered to help but he has drunk too much and can barely stand. It will be a long time, I think, before he gets over what happened." He stood. "How about if I meet you in front of the tavern at midnight?"

Fargo agreed and Hetsutu left. Unfriendly glares followed him out but no one said anything, which was just as well.

The time passed slowly. By eleven only a few customers were left. Liana shooed them out, shut the door and threw the bolt, and sashayed to his table wearing a come-hither grin.

"Finally. I couldn't wait to be alone with you." She sat on the edge of the table and moved her leg enticingly. "Suppose we take up where we left off when you went off monster hunting?"

"Speaking of the boar," Fargo said, and related the plan to stand watch.

"But now I must wait even longer." Liana pouted, then glanced at the clock above the bar. "Still, midnight isn't for an hour yet. Give me a few minutes to wash up."

"What's your rush?" Fargo put his hand on her shin and traced his fingers up under her dress.

"I told you before. Not in here. In the back."

Ignoring her, Fargo ran his hand to her knee. Her skin was warm and smooth.

"I refuse to do it on this table."

Fargo's fingers molded her thigh. "Are you sure I can't change your mind?"

"I do so like when you do that," Liana said huskily. "You make me tingle all over."

Fargo inched his hand higher and she parted her legs.

"Men!"

"You love it and you know it." Fargo moved his chair so there was room on his lap. "Have a seat."

"Are you forgetting my nice, soft comfortable bed?"

"We'll get there eventually."

"If it—" Liana stopped at a knock on the front door. "Go away! I'm closed for the night!"

The knock was repeated.

"Didn't you hear me? I'm closed."

Whoever was out there rapped a third time, harder than ever.

"Some people just don't listen." Liana marched over and threw the bolt.

"I have half a mind to—" She stopped. "Goodness. What are you doing out this late?"

Fargo heard someone reply but so quietly he couldn't hear what they said. Then Liana stepped back and two small figures entered. "What the hell?" he blurted.

Clovis and Halette appeared nervous. The boy had his Sharps and the girl was wringing her hands. They came straight over.

"Monsieur Fargo, we're sorry to bother you but when we went to find Uncle Remy, the Breed told us he is half drunk."

"Hetsutu," Fargo said.

"What?"

"The Breed has a name. It's Hetsutu. You might want to use it from now on."

Halette stepped up and placed her hand on his arm. "We're awful worried and we don't know what to do."

"About what? And where's your father? Shouldn't you be telling him this?"

"That's just it," Clovis said. "It's him we're worried about."

"He left us."

"What are you talking about? Where would he go at this time of night?"

"Into the swamp," Halette said.

Fargo was dumbfounded.

"Someone brought word about the Mad Indian," Clovis said. "Papa holds him partly to blame for Mama's death so he tucked us into bed and told us he would be back in the morning and for us not to worry."

"He went into the swamp," Halette said again, and trembled with fright. "I begged him not to but he wouldn't listen."

A slew of cuss words were on the tip of Fargo's tongue. Instead he said, "The damned fool."

"Will you go after him?" Halette pleaded. "He shouldn't be out there alone."

"He shouldn't be out there at all."

"I wouldn't know where to start looking."

"For me. I don't want to lose him too." Tears welled in Halette's eyes.

Clovis put his arm around her. "Don't cry. If he won't do it, we'll go look for Papa ourselves."

Fargo had to let it out. "Son of a bitch."

13

The swamp, as Hetsutu had said, was unusually still.

And sure enough, one of the pirogues was missing.

Fargo stood gazing into the dark and debating whether to take the other pirogue and go after Namo or stay put and wait for Namo to return. To find him out there would be next to impossible. But he'd promised Halette and Clovis he would try so he cupped a hand to his mouth and bellowed Namo's name on the chance Namo was within earshot.

There was no reply.

Fargo had less than an hour before he was to meet Hetsutu in front of the tavern. He'd left the kids with Liana and told her that if he wasn't back by midnight to let Hetsutu know where he had gone.

Placing his Henry in the bottom of the second pirogue, Fargo pushed until it floated free, climbed in, picked up a paddle, and was under way. He stroked as quietly as he could, wending among the moss-laden cypress. He had gone only a short way when he stopped paddling and coasted. A glance back confirmed he could still see the lights of the settlement.

Fargo wasn't about to venture much farther. Even with his keen sense of direction he could easily become lost. Landmarks were hard to recognize at night, even more so in a swamp where everything was mired in murk and the dark tangle of waterways was a maze.

Again Fargo cupped a hand to his mouth and hollered. Again there was no answer.

"Damn it."

Fargo let the pirogue drift. He was about to call out

once more when he heard a shrill cry. Not the squeal of the razorback, but the thin bleat of something much smaller. He heard it a second time, off to his left, and used the paddle. It was an animal in distress. That there weren't any snarls or growls suggested a predator wasn't to blame. But you never knew.

Another cry, much closer, prompted Fargo to pick up his Henry. He was drifting toward a mound covered mostly with grass. He couldn't make out much about it other than that there appeared to be something on top of the mound, something alive, something that was frantically jumping up and down.

Whatever it was, it wasn't any bigger than a cat.

The pirogue bumped to a stop. Fargo expected the animal to bolt but it stopped jumping and stared down at him, its eyes dim gleams in the starlight. Climbing out, he moved toward it. Instantly, the animal erupted in a frenzy of hopping and bleats of terror.

Fargo bent and saw what it was. But what he was seeing made no sense.

Someone had caught a rabbit and tied it to a stake. Held fast by a rawhide cord around its neck, the rabbit shrieked and tried desperately to bound off.

Fargo stepped back, thinking that would quiet it, but the rabbit only screeched louder. The only purpose he could come up with for staking it there was as bait. But bait for what? he wondered. For a fox? A cougar? An alligator, maybe? And where was the hunter who had staked the rabbit out?

Then, from the benighted swamp beyond, floated a very human laugh. Not loud, or long, but enough that Fargo could tell that the person laughing wasn't quite sane.

The Mad Indian.

It had to be. But that meant the lunatic had staked out the rabbit. Fargo sought some sign of the madman and happened to glance toward the settlement. The lights were plainly visible. Much more so than when he had been among the cypress.

An awful idea came over him.

Fargo tried to remember everything he knew about wild hogs, and razorbacks in particular. Their diet consisted of just about anything and everything. They were partial to acorns and roots and tubers. They liked berries and fruit and sometimes ate grass. They also liked meat. Razorbacks, in fact, were known to devour all kinds of living things: frogs, snakes, birds, even fawns. He'd heard tell that the succulent flesh of young rabbits was a favorite. Razorbacks had been known to root out rabbit warrens just to get at the young ones.

Fargo looked at the rabbit. It appeared young to him.

And then from the dark came a grunt and a squeal.

There was no time to lose. Fargo yanked on the stake but it refused to budge. It had been pounded in too deep. He put down the Henry, gripped it with both hands, and tried again.

The rabbit was in a panic. It flopped wildly about and screamed—if its cries could be called that. But whatever they were called, they served their purpose.

A thousand pounds of sinew and gristle was bearing down on that mound, The razorback was coming to feed.

"Damn," Fargo hissed, and tugged harder. He could try to dig the stake out but that would take too long. Then it hit him. "What the hell am I doing?" Quickly, he slid his hand into his boot and drew the Arkansas toothpick. A single slash was all it took to sever the cord.

In a twinkling the rabbit was gone. It flew down the mound and leaped into the water and swam with amazing speed—straight into a living mountain. Jaw snapped and bone crunched and the rabbit shrieked one last time.

Whirling and snatching up the Henry, Fargo sprang for the pirogue. He bumped his shin climbing in. Grabbing the paddle, he pushed off and started to turn the pirogue toward Gros Ville. A squeal and loud splashing from the other side of the mound warned him he was out of time.

Fargo stroked toward a cypress choked with a spidery veil of moss that hung clear down to the water. He barely got behind it in time. Parting the moss, he saw the huge mass of the boar appear atop the mound.

The razorback raised its snout to the sky. It sniffed loudly, then grunted and moved in small circles. The stake drew its interest. The boar tore at it with its tusks.

Fargo held his breath, not daring to move. If the boar caught his scent it would be on him before he could get out of there.

The razorback stopped rooting. It gazed about and stared directly at the moss screening Fargo. Could the thing see him? It was his understanding that hogs and pigs couldn't see any better than humans but he could be wrong.

With a loud grunt, the razorback came down the near side of the mound to the water. Not twenty feet separated the beast from Fargo's hiding place. He waited, every nerve raw.

Tilting its huge head, the boar sniffed some more. It seemed about to plunge in and come toward him when it suddenly turned.

It had seen the lights.

Surely not, Fargo thought. Surely it would realize what Gros Ville was. But if so, either it didn't care— or in its perpetual fury it was so bloodthirsty that all it could think of was killing. Snorting, it barreled into the water, heading for the settlement.

Fargo had to warn them. He brought the pirogue into the open. Already the razorback was almost out of sight. Swiftly, he traded the paddle for the Henry, jammed the stock to his shoulder, and banged off three shots. He had no hope of killing it but that wasn't his intention. He was trying to turn it, to make it come after him instead of attacking Gros Ville.

The razorback didn't stop.

Fargo put down the rifle and paddled with all his might. He flew as fast as one man could but it wasn't anywhere near fast enough. He hoped against hope that something would divert it, or that the smells and the sounds would cause it to retreat into the swamp. Most razorbacks would. But this one wasn't like most. This one was a berserk killer, as mad as the Mad Indian. It wasn't going to stop.

The Cajuns would be talking about this night for years to come.

Fargo still was hundreds of yards out when the first scream pierced the night. A scream followed by the boar's shrill squeals. And then more screams, and shots, and the crash of a wall. A ruckus this side of bedlam. He saw figures running wildly about, saw muzzle flashes and heard men swear.

His shoulder throbbed and his arms ached but Fargo threw himself into stroking with renewed vigor. Flames lent incentive. A lamp or a lantern had been knocked over and one of the buildings was on fire. As dry as everything was, the fire would spread swiftly.

Fargo thought of Halette and Liana and Clovis, and swore. He was a stone's throw from the shore when a small girl broke from between two buildings, screaming hysterically. For a few dreadful moments he thought it was Halette, but no, it was some other girl, and hard after her thundered the razorback. He grabbed the Henry.

A man appeared, standing straight and tall between the charging boar and the girl. Flickering light from the spreading fire revealed who it was.

"No!" Fargo yelled. "Get out of there!"

If Hetsutu heard, he gave no indication. Instead he raised his rifle and fired.

The razorback squealed but didn't veer aside. Hetsutu fired again, and yet a third time, taking precise aim. But if his shots scored they had no effect.

"Run!"

Hetsutu tried to spring aside. He coiled his legs and leaped but he wasn't more than a foot off the ground when the razorback rammed into him. Fargo expected to see him go flying, but no, one of the boar's tusks hooked deep. The razorback stopped and tossed its head from side to side, squealing all the while.

There was nothing Fargo could do. He took a bead but he didn't have a clear shot. He had to watch in helpless horror as the boar ripped and mangled Hetsutu.

Hetsutu never cried out. Limbs flapping, his body slid free and dropped.

Fargo heard the thud as clear as anything.

The girl had reached the canoes and the pirogues and had the presence of mind to climb into a canoe and flatten.

Snorting and sniffing, the razorback came after her.

Fargo sighted on its head. He was on the verge of firing when somewhere a woman screamed and the razorback wheeled and raced in her direction.

The pirogue crunched onto solid ground. Fargo dashed to the canoe to find the little girl quaking and sniffling, the whites of her eyes showing.

"Stay put. You're as safe here as anywhere. I'll come back for you."

The girl said something in French.

"What?"

"The beast, monsieur! It killed my mother! It came through our wall as if the wall were made of paper!"

Fargo ran after it. He had no plan other than to try and keep it from killing anyone else. Suddenly he stopped.

Hetsutu's ruptured body lay practically at his feet. Most of Hetsutu's organs were no longer in the body. From the abdominal cavity oozed the intestines, like so many coils of a snake. Several ribs had been shattered and one poked through the flesh.

Fargo poured on speed. He came to the street, and to chaos run rampant.

Several buildings were aflame. People were running every which way, shouting and bawling and bellowing. Bodies lay sprawled in violent death. Two of the shacks had been flattened and from under the broken roof of one of them came the shrill sobs of a woman.

"Help me! Please help me!"

From under the other shack protruded a bloody arm.

A Cajun ran up, a man Fargo had never seen before, and clutched at his shirt. "Have you seen him?"

"Who?"

"My son. He is only six. He ran off and I can't find him."

Fargo shook his head and the distraught man ran off. That reminded him. He ran to the tavern. It appeared to be intact and wasn't on fire. But the front door hung wide open.

Dashing in, Fargo cast about for Liana and the children. He called their names. Fear filled him when he got no answer.

Fargo ran back out. They had to be there somewhere. He took a few strides and was brought up short when a breathless Remy Cuvier materialized out of the smoke and the mayhem.

Remy was armed with a rifle and pistols. His eyes were bloodshot and he reeked of alcohol.

"Here you are! I have been looking for you and Namo and the Breed. Have you seen them?"

"Hetsutu is dead."

Remy took a step back. "*Non!* Say it isn't so."

"I saw it with my own eyes."

"He was my best friend. My right arm."

"Namo is off in the swamp—"

"What's that? The fool!"

"His kids are with the woman who owns the tavern—"

"Liana. Yes, I know her."

"Help me find them." Fargo made off up the street. Whether Remy did or didn't tag along, he must make sure they were safe.

Flames engulfed a building on the right. A number of men were trying to put out the fire but the few buckets they had weren't enough. A body lay so close to a burning wall that no one could risk pulling it away.

The body was Doucet's. A tusk had ripped his jaw and part of his face off.

Fargo shouted Liana's name. He shouted Halette's. "Damn it. Where are they?"

"They could be anywhere."

A cloud of smoke wafted over them. Fargo got it into his eyes and into his lungs. Coughing, he turned to one side.

"The beast! Look!"

The razorback was attacking another shack. In a mindless rage, it slammed into a plank wall again and again.

"Here is our chance to kill it!"

The boar chose that moment to turn—and saw them. Squealing fiercely, it charged.

"Oh hell!" Remy said.

14

Fargo and Remy both snapped up their rifles.

The razorback was closing rapidly when two Cajuns came running around the corner of a building, saw it, and opened fire. Instantly the razorback veered toward them. Fargo swore their shots hit it but the lead had no effect. With astounding speed the boar was on them. Those twin tusks ripped once, ripped twice, and writhing bodies were left in the beast's wake.

Fargo went to shoot but the razorback raced around the corner and was gone.

"That thing is a devil!" Remy exclaimed.

Fargo was thinking of Liana and the children. There was no sign of them along the entire street. On a hunch, he ran back toward the tavern. All around was a riot of confusion as Cajuns fought fires or tended to screaming wounded or wept over dead ones. He heard the squeals of the razorback but from a ways off.

"What are we doing?" Remy asked.

Fargo barreled into the tavern. Once more he shouted their names, half-fearing they had rushed out when the boar first attacked and might be lying out there somewhere, torn and bleeding.

Then a voice answered. From out of the back they came, Liana with her arms around Halette and Clovis. They ran to him and Halette threw her arms around his legs while Liana hugged him.

"*Mon Dieu!* I was so worried! We heard cries and we looked out and saw the monster coming down the street, attacking everyone it passed. So I took them to my bedroom and we hid under the bed."

Halette was sobbing.

"We thought we heard you a while ago and came out but you weren't here," Liana said.

"Where is our papa?" Clovis asked. "Did you find him?"

"Still out in the swamp." Fargo didn't add "and maybe dead" but he was thinking it.

Liana gave a start and recoiled, her hand over her mouth. She was staring at the doorway.

Fargo figured Remy had come in but when he turned it was a Cajun woman holding the limp body of a small boy. A tusk had caught the boy in the neck and his small head hung by shreds. Quickly, Fargo scooped Halette up and held her so she couldn't see.

"Simone!" Liana hurried to her.

Clovis said, "We must find Papa." And before anyone could stop him, he dashed past Liana and past the stricken mother and out into the night.

"Get back here!" Fargo hollered, and heard a yelp. He darted around the women and out the door.

"Let go of me!"

Remy had hold of Clovis's arm. "Calm down, boy. You're not going anywhere with that *bête* out there."

"But my papa is out there, too!"

"He's a grown man. You're not." Remy shook him to quiet him. "Do you think I don't know how you feel? Your mother was my cousin, was she not? And a good friend, besides. I loved her, boy. And I swear to you by all that is holy, that beast will pay for her death, as it will for the death of my friends." He pushed Clovis toward Fargo.

Squeals came from the swamp but from far off.

The glow from the burning buildings lit a scene of slaughter and destruction. Shouts and wails rose on all sides. Those who were not hurt were helping those who were. Bodies were being covered. And not only humans had suffered. Two horses and a dog were down, one horse kicking in its own entrails.

"It's a nightmare," Remy said.

Fargo couldn't get over how much damage the razorback had caused, or how many it had killed and maimed. Granted, it was a thousand pounds of muscle and ferocity, but still. He was more determined than ever to hunt the thing down and slay it. It, and the madman that used it as a tool of revenge on those the madman blamed for the deaths of his people.

Fargo put Halette down. "I want you and your brother to go to Liana's room and stay there."

"I'll do no such thing," Clovis said. "I want to help you look for my papa."

"First things first."

Remy used his boot on the boy's bottom. "Do as he tells you. This is not the time to argue."

They went down the street to the landing. Faint in the distance they could hear the razorback.

"Tomorrow I go after it," Remy said.

"You won't be alone." Fargo went to the canoe where he had left the girl but she was gone. "Damn." He hoped she hadn't blundered into the boar's path a second time.

Smoke drifted over them, wispy tendrils writhing like fog.

Motioning to Remy, Fargo led him to where Hetsutu lay. "I figured we would bury him ourselves."

His head bowed, Remy sank to his knees. "I thank you but it is mine to do. Of all my friends he was the best."

"I'll be at the tavern."

But Fargo had barely taken two steps when the swish of a paddle heralded a pirogue gliding out of the gloom. He moved to meet it.

Namo stopped stroking and let the canoe glide to a stop. He sat glued in astonishment, taking in the devastation. "How can this be?"

"You haven't seen the worst yet."

Putting down the paddle, Namo climbed out. Fargo helped him pull the pirogue out of the water.

"I heard the beast and the screams and came as fast as I could. I kept telling myself it was impossible, that the boar wouldn't dare." Namo started up the street, walking as one in a daze. Then he stiffened and blurted, "My children?"

"Safe at the tavern."

Namo broke into a run and Fargo paced him. They passed a man cradling a woman. The horse had stopped thrashing but was still breathing with the rasp of a blacksmith's bellows. The acrid smell of smoke mixed with the pungent odor of blood and gore.

"That I should live to witness such a thing," Namo said softly. "Who would have thought the razorback would—" He didn't finish.

"It wasn't by chance." Fargo told him about the part the Mad Indian played.

Namo stopped cold. "You saw the rabbit and stake with your own eyes? Then the lunatic is as much to blame as the boar." He smacked a hand against his leg. "I've just had a thought. What if the Mad Indian had a hand in the deaths of some of those who have gone missing? What if he somehow lured the razorback to them as he lured it here?"

"Anything is possible."

"All this time we thought we were up against just an animal but the man must be slain, too."

"Where we find one we're likely to find the other."

The rest of the night crawled by. Liana let the children sleep in her bed. Fargo spread out his blankets out back next to the Ovaro, the Henry at his side, the Colt in his hand. He didn't sleep well. He kept hearing screams and squeals and waking up in a cold sweat. The last time, a pink tinge to the east signified dawn would soon break, and he got up and bundled his bedroll and went into the tavern to put coffee on.

Someone had beaten him to the kitchen.

"*Bonjour*," Remy Cuvier said from over at the table. He lifted a steaming cup. "*Comment allez-vous?*"

"If you're asking me how I am," Fargo said as he stepped to the stove, "I feel about the same as you look."

"You couldn't sleep either?" Remy took a slow sip. "I doubt I will ever again have a good night's rest."

Fargo filled a cup and joined him. "I'd like to get an early start. One of us should wake Namo."

"No need," said the gent in question as he entered with a pack over his shoulder. "I have been lying in the bedroom for the past hour staring at the ceiling and finally couldn't take it anymore."

"We need to have words, you and I," Remy said.

"I know what you are going to say and you can't talk me out of it."

"Hear me out. Your wife was one of the kindest women I knew. She didn't turn her back on me as most of my family did. For that I owe her."

Namo began slicing a loaf of bread. "Nothing you can say will change my mind."

"Damn it, man. Think of your children. If something were to happen to you, where would that leave them? Orphans. With no one to look after them." Remy wagged a finger at him. "If you care for them, you'll stay here. Fargo and I can get by without you."

"Who are you trying to fool? Just the two of you against that beast and the Mad Indian? You can use a third set of eyes and a third rifle."

"But Clovis and sweet Halette—"

"I've talked it over with them. They understand. Should I share my wife's fate, they will go live with my brother. He will gladly take them in."

"So I am wasting my breath?"

"*Oui.*"

Fargo didn't contribute but he agreed with Remy. They finished their coffee in silence. Namo slung his pack, urged them to be quiet so as not to awaken his children, and they filed down the hall.

Three figures awaited them at the front door.

"Were you going to leave without saying good-bye, Papa?" Halette asked accusingly.

Namo stared hard at Liana. "This is your doing."

Clovis stepped between them. "No, it's not, Papa. Halette and I thought you would try to slip away so we took turns staying awake and I woke her when you went to the kitchen."

"I did not want a scene."

Liana said, "Better tears now than have your daughter cry all day because her father was too callous to hug her when he left."

"That is harsh."

Remy nudged Fargo. "This is not for us, eh? Let's wait for him at the pirogues."

Fargo nodded. But first he went up to Clovis and held out his Henry. "I'd like to swap you."

"Monsieur?"

"I want to use your Sharps. You can hold on to my rifle until I get back." Left unsaid was the fact that if Fargo didn't make it back, the boy could keep the Henry.

Clovis glanced at Namo. "Papa?"

"It is your decision. The Sharps is yours."

"I guess I will do it, then," Clovis said uncertainly, and they switched. He ran a hand over the shiny brass receiver. "This is the prettiest gun I have ever seen."

"How much spare ammo do you have for this?"

"Eleven cartridges." Clovis untied a pouch from his belt and held it out. "I'm sorry it isn't more."

Fargo jiggled the pouch, opened it, and took one out. It was longer and thicker than the cartridges for his Henry. But then the Henry was a .44 caliber and the Sharps was a .52. "These will have to do me." All it should take was one shot to the right spot. "I'm obliged."

Gros Ville looked as if it had been through a war. Wisps of smoke rose from the charred remains of the buildings that had burned to the ground. The two flattened shacks were in shambles. Bodies had been removed but blood stains marked where the victims had fallen.

Few of the inhabitants were out and about. An old man sat under an overhang, weeping. A woman was shuffling about saying someone's name over and over again.

Remy crossed himself.

A surprise awaited them at the landing. Eight men were already there, loading supplies.

"What is this?"

"Need you ask?" a burly Cajun replied. "We are going after the beast. We can't permit a repeat of last night."

Remy nodded at Fargo and Namo. "Why not leave it to me and my friends?"

"*Non*," the burly Cajun said. "What sort of men would we be to let others fight our battles?"

A sour-faced Cajun swore and spat. "My wife had her arm ripped open by that thing. Only her arm, so in that we were lucky. But I vowed to her that I will kill the brute."

A third one gazed at the bleak ruin of their settlement. "We must defend what is ours."

Fargo realized there was no talking them out of it, and he didn't try. He did say, "There's something you should keep in mind. The razorback didn't show up here by chance. The Mad Indian lured him."

"What are you saying, monsieur? That the monster is the Mad Indian's pet?"

At that, some of them laughed.

"Don't mock him," Remy growled. "If he says it is so, it is."

"Now I have heard everything," the surly Cajun said. "You, of all people, trust an outsider?"

With two men to a craft, the avengers pushed off.

"They're fools," Remy declared.

"What does that make us?" Fargo wondered.

15

The great swamp was as oppressive as ever. Shadowy gloom held sway where the canopy was thickest. Occasional patches of sunlight gave a luster to the gator- and snake-infested water it didn't deserve.

The swamp was a world unto itself. A hostile world. A world that would kill the unwary in the blink of an eye.

Fargo sat in the stern of the pirogue, paddling. Remy was in the bow, Namo in the middle. They sat tensely, eyes constantly probing the vegetation and the water, their rifles across their legs. It was nearing midday and the sun was nearly directly overhead.

"I used to love the swamp but now I hate it," Remy broke their long quiet. "It is a foul place."

Namo said, "Despite all that has happened, I will always love it. To me it is my home."

Remy nodded at a cottonmouth that was slithering away from their craft. "To that it is home. To us it will always be alien. We will always be intruders. Unwelcome intruders."

"There is a beauty to the swamp," Namo insisted. "One must look beneath the surface to appreciate it."

"Look beneath the surface and you will find an alligator ready to bite your head off or a water moccasin ready to strike."

Fargo didn't get involved in their argument. He understood both points of view. To him, the swamp was a festering quagmire. Yet he could see why Namo liked it as much as he liked the mountains and the prairie.

"We should stop soon and rest," Namo proposed. "No sense in tiring ourselves out our first day."

They were gliding along somber ranks of cypress, the trees spaced far enough apart that they had an easy going. That soon changed. Before them rose one of the intermittent tracts of land that broke the monotony, this one several acres in extent. Remy made for a point where the ground sloped. Hopping out, they hauled the pirogue out.

Namo carried the pack to a grassy spot. "This looks safe enough."

Fargo didn't sit when they did. His leg muscles were cramped and he paced to relieve the pain.

"How do we even know the razorback came this way?" Remy said.

"This is the direction it was heading when we heard it last."

"But we've seen no sign of it. No sign at all."

Namo was opening the pack. "I suspect it sticks to the water. But we're bound to find something." He indicated the rank growth. "It could be hiding in there for all we know."

"After we kill it I am leaving the Atchafalaya."

"You don't mean that," Namo said in surprise. "You have lived here your whole life."

"And what has it gotten me? I'm an outcast, shunned by my own kind. All my friends are dead."

"I'm your friend."

"You know what I mean. Life was bearable so long as I had other outcasts to share it with."

"Where will you go?"

"New Orleans, I think. I've been there a few times and there is much about it I like."

"You won't last a month," Namo predicted. "City life isn't for the likes of you. Or me, for that matter."

Fargo was listening for sounds of wildlife but there weren't any. Not so much as the chirp of a bird. That struck him as peculiar. Moving a few feet from the others, he peered into the growth.

"I'm not you," Remy said to Namo. "You have the swamp in your blood. I merely tolerate it."

"My offer holds. You can come and live with us if you like. My children adore you."

Remy looked away and was a while answering. When he did, his voice had a husky quality. "I thank you. The three of you are the only people left in this world who truly care about me. But no, my friend. Think of what others would say. The talk. The gossip. I am not held in high regard." He chuckled. "To put it mildly."

"What do I care what other people think? So you are an outcast. You have never killed a Cajun."

"That I would never do."

"Then let people say what they will. There are always small minds and loose tongues."

Remy smiled. "I can see what my cousin saw in you, Namo Heuse. You have a fine quality."

"I pull my pants on one leg at a time like every other man. But I won't be swayed by the opinions of others."

Fargo was listening with half an ear. He was more interested in why the spit of land was so empty of life. He was about to say something when he gazed at the high grass a few yards behind Remy and Namo and a tingle of alarm shot down his spine. "Look out!" he hollered, while simultaneously jerking the Sharps to his shoulder.

The two Cajuns reacted with razor reflexes and sprang to their feet.

Out of the grass hurtled an alligator six feet long, or so. It snapped at Remy, its razor teeth narrowly missing his leg. Its own legs pumping, it dived into the water with a loud splash. Bubbles rose, marking its underwater course, and then stopped.

Remy cursed luridly. "Did you see? It almost had me. It is an omen. I must get out of this swamp while I still can."

"That could have happened to anyone," Namo said, eyeing the surface with his rifle up.

"Here, yes. But you don't see many alligators wandering the streets of New Orleans."

Fargo had come to a decision. "I'm going to scout around. It could be the boar was here."

"You shouldn't go alone," Namo said.

"I'll give a holler if I need you." Fargo penetrated the tangle, moving slowly, treading with care, watchful for snakes and other gators. A mosquito buzzed him but flew off. Then a butterfly flitted by, a splash of color, reminding him the world wasn't all gloom.

Fargo came on a game trail. He sank to one knee to examine it. Deer tracks were plentiful. In a patch of dirt he also found the prints of a skunk and a raccoon. Farther on he saw bobcat tracks. He rounded a bend and drew up short.

There, plain as could be, were different hoofprints. They were larger than the deer tracks, and more rounded. The dewclaws were longer, and more pointed. Only one animal made those kind of tracks.

Wild boar.

Fargo looked up, his skin prickling. He almost called out to Remy and Namo. But the tracks were fresh. The animal might be near. He didn't think it was the razorback; the tracks weren't big enough.

The quiet took on new meaning.

Fargo wedged the Sharps to his shoulder and kept going. It could be the tracks were those of a sow. And it could be the razorback was paying her a visit. Male boar were as randy as an animal could be.

The trail was as sinuous as a snake, turning and twisting every which way. Suddenly it ended at the last thing Fargo expected to find: a spring. Edging close, he touched his left hand to the water and let a drop fall on the tip of his tongue. It tasted clean and cool.

The spring explained all the tracks. It explained what the wild boars were doing there.

Another trail led to the spring on the other side. Dense growth was everywhere else.

Fargo scoured the vegetation but saw nothing. He lowered the Sharps, cupped his palm, and dipped his

113

hand in. He raised his palm to his mouth and drank. He dipped his hand again, drank again. Somewhere off in the swamp a frog croaked. He wondered why there were no frogs at the spring. He dipped his hand in a third time, and froze.

An eyeball was staring back at him.

Fargo pretended not to notice. He looked past it and then roved his gaze back again.

The eyeball was fixed on him unblinkingly.

Only then did Fargo realize that what he took for shadow wasn't shadow at all but a large animal. The silhouette left no doubt as to what it was. Either a boar or a sow. It wasn't the giant razorback but that hardly mattered. *Any* wild boar that size could kill.

Calmly, Fargo sipped from his palm. The Sharps was at his side. If he snapped it up the boar might charge. Since it wasn't the one they were after he would as soon let it live. He began to back away and to slowly raise the Sharps, just in case.

Fargo didn't think to look over his shoulder, which made his surprise all the greater when a squeal came from behind him. He glanced back and saw two young boars, or piglets, which told him the large animal in the brush was a sow and these were her offspring.

"Oh, hell."

With a savage squeal the sow burst into the open. She had her head up and her mouth wide.

Fargo dived out of her way. She bit at him but missed and went on by. Rolling onto his shoulder, he took a quick bead but the sow hadn't turned to attack him again. She was racing down the trail with her young.

Rising, Fargo waited a suitable interval, then started back. He was extra cautious. Where there was one sow there were often more. The females lived in groups known as sounders. If Fargo recollected rightly, there could be anywhere from a dozen or so up to fifty animals in one sounder. Only females and young. The males kept to themselves except when mating.

The last thing Fargo needed was to run into twenty or thirty at once.

He had no trouble finding the spot where the Cajuns and the pirogue should be—only they weren't there.

Fargo looked around in bewilderment. He refused to believe they had up and left him. He went to shout but thought better of it. Hunkering, he waited. All sorts of wild imaginings went through his head. What if they had seen the razorback and gone after it? Or spotted the Mad Indian and gone after him? And what if they never came back? It would take him months to find his way out of the swamp, if he even made it.

Out on the water another cottonmouth appeared, coming in his direction.

"Swamps," Fargo said in disgust. He picked up a stick and threw it. He missed, but the stick hit close enough that the cottonmouth turned and swam away. "Good riddance."

A peculiar call came out of the cypress. A bird, Fargo reckoned, although it could well be a person imitating a bird. The Mad Indian, maybe.

To say Fargo was relieved when he saw the pirogue glide into view was an understatement. Standing, he controlled his temper and simply said once they were in earshot, "I don't much like you going off without telling me."

Namo was in the bow. "My apologies, *mon ami*. But you were taking so long, we thought we could put the time to good use."

"That's right," Remy said. "We were looking for sign of the razorback but didn't see him."

"We did find evidence of other boars."

"They're here," Fargo confirmed. "I saw a female and her young."

The Cajuns brought the pirogue broadside to the shoreline so he could climb in.

"It could be the razorback will show up here eventually," Remy said. "So the question is, do we wait or do we push on?"

"We push on," Namo said. "It might be days or weeks before he shows, if ever."

Fargo agreed with Heuse.

As they rounded the spit of land the underbrush crackled and out rushed several large sows. Squealing angrily, they pawed the dirt and showed their teeth but didn't plunge into the water in pursuit.

Remy chuckled.

"What can you possibly find humorous about them?" Namo wanted to know.

"To a male boar they are beauties."

Ahead was another dark cypress grove.

Swarms of what Fargo took to be gnats descended. He could hardly breathe without getting some into his nose or his mouth. To ward them off he covered the lower half of his face with his bandana.

Remy started muttering.

"What bothers you?" Namo asked.

"This is a waste of our time. We could hunt forever and not find the razorback."

"Are you saying we should sit around Gros Ville and do nothing?"

"*Non.* I am saying we should do this smart. Maybe the Mad Indian is not so mad, after all."

"You've lost me."

"He lured the razorback to the settlement, didn't he? Perhaps we should do the same and lure it to us."

"How do you propose doing that?"

"We camp and make a lot of noise so that it can hear us or smell us," Remy proposed. "If nothing else—" He suddenly stopped.

"If nothing else what?"

When Remy didn't answer, Fargo glanced at him and saw that his attention was fixed on something off to their left. He looked, and blurted, "Speak of the devil."

It was the Mad Indian.

16

"We can't let him get away!" Namo Heuse shouted, and brought up his rifle to shoot.

But the Mad Indian was already fleeing. He had spotted them at the same instant they spotted him and he was working his paddle furiously, heading his canoe deeper into the swamp.

The crack of Namo's rifle galvanized Remy into working his own paddle. "You missed."

So it seemed. The Mad Indian had bent low and was stroking with amazing swiftness for a man his age. He glanced back and gave voice to that insane cackle of his.

"He must pay for my wife," Namo said grimly as he set down his rifle and scooped up his paddle.

Fargo was waiting for a clear shot. They were in among cypress and the Mad Indian was using that to his advantage, wending right and left among the trees so there was nearly always a tree between his canoe and their pirogue. Twice Fargo fixed a bead but each time a tree trunk or trailing moss thwarted him.

"Do you know what this means?" Remy said. "If the Mad Indian is near, the razorback must be near, too."

Fargo was keeping an eye out for it. But the boar had an uncanny knack for attacking unexpectedly and might be on them before he could put a slug into it.

The Mad Indian kept on cackling.

Remy swore. "He gives me chills, that one."

Namo was hunched forward as if he would dive over the bow. "He is nothing but a crazy old man."

"Crazy, *oui*. But for all we know God is on his side and not ours."

Fargo and Namo both glanced back.

"Since when do you care about God?" Namo asked. "And how can you say something like that? It's ridiculous."

"Is it?" Remy countered. "The Mad Indian's people were wiped out by disease brought by white men. In God's eyes maybe we are in the wrong and he is in the right."

Namo shook his head. "I can't believe I'm hearing this. Next you will tell me you want to go to confession and make amends for all your sins."

"I am only saying," Remy said. "And just because I have killed and like to drink and indulge in women doesn't mean I am completely without faith."

"Bah. After what happened to Emmeline, I have begun to doubt there even is a God. She did nothing to deserve dying like she did."

Fargo interrupted them. "Less talk and more paddling."

The Mad Indian was widening his lead. He was one man to their three but his canoe was smaller and lighter than the pirogue and he was amazingly strong for a bundle of sinew and bone.

"He is making fools of us," Namo said, and increased his speed.

Fargo continued to stay alert for the razorback.

The Mad Indian's teeth flashed and his laughter carried to them along with, "Mad, mad, mad, mad, mad!"

"As if we don't know that," Namo rasped.

"He is taunting us," Remy stated the obvious. "Rubbing our noses in what we have driven him to."

"Don't start with that again. He can't possibly be in the right. Not with all the people he has had that monster pig of his kill."

"I just had a thought," Remy said.

"Not another one."

"What if he raised it? What if the Mad Indian raised that razorback? Some Indians raise hogs, do they not?"

"*Oui*. But you've seen the razorback. It is no hog.

118

It's a wild boar. As wild as they come. It would as soon turn on the Mad Indian as attack us."

"But sometimes wild boars come close to Indian villages to forage for food," Remy persisted. "It could be there is more to the razorback and the Mad Indian than we suspect."

"You are full of silly thoughts today."

"Go to hell, Namo."

After that they paddled in silence. Fargo stayed out of it. The way he saw things, whether the Mad Indian did or didn't raise the razorback was irrelevant. The orgy of death and terror must be stopped.

To their collective chagrin, they were falling farther behind. Namo and Remy paddled harder but it did no good.

"We'll never catch him," Remy declared.

"Don't give up."

"Did I say I would?"

The Mad Indian swept around a cypress and didn't reappear.

"Where did he get to?" Namo wondered.

"Paddle, damn you."

They flew past the same tree. Spread before them was a small island, an oasis of growth so thick as to appear impenetrable. On the shore, half in and half out of the water, bobbed the Mad Indian's canoe, the paddle lying on the ground a few feet away.

"We have him!" Namo cried.

No sooner were the words out of his mouth than an arrow streaked out of the foliage. Namo had no time to react but he was lucky—the shaft struck his paddle and was deflected.

Fargo drew his Colt and banged off two quick shots, firing at the spot the arrow came from. More cackling greeted the blasts.

"You missed," Remy said.

The pirogue lurched to a stop next to the canoe and the three of them piled out, seeking cover.

Fargo flattened behind a log and replaced the spent cartridges. The undergrowth was ominously still.

Namo whispered his name to get his attention. "One of us must stay here to keep the madman from getting away while the other two go in after him."

"I'm not staying," Remy said, and before they could think to stop him, he rose and plunged into the vegetation.

"What is the matter with him today?" Namo asked. Without waiting for an answer, he went in after him.

Fargo swore. He was the one who should go; he was the better tracker. Shoving the Colt into his holster, he rested the Sharps's barrel on the log and scoured the greenery.

A troubling thought struck him. What if the Mad Indian picked that island for a reason? In the dense tangle the madman could easily pick them off.

A fly buzzed his ear.

A centipede crawled along the log.

The quiet was unnerving.

Fargo kept expecting to hear a shout or a shot. He did hear a slight sound behind him in the water, and twisted. The barest of ripples disturbed the surface. A fish or a snake, he reckoned, and faced the vegetation.

A bird screeched.

A cricket chirped.

Another sound behind him made Fargo turn his head a second time. There were more ripples. Small ones. The same fish or snake or maybe a frog or turtle, he figured.

The minutes crawled.

Fargo thought he heard voices. Then, from far off, Remy yelled his name. Quickly rising, Fargo ran a dozen yards in. "Where are you?"

Remy yelled again but it was impossible to tell what he was saying.

"I can't hear you! What's wrong?"

Again Remy shouted but only one word was clear. "Slipped."

"I still didn't hear you!"

"Watch out! We think he slipped past us into the swamp!"

"The swamp?" Fargo repeated. Why would the Mad Indian go into the swamp on foot? The answer hit him like a five-ton boulder. Whirling, he flew back to the pirogue and the canoe—only they weren't there.

Forty feet out the Mad Indian, only his head and arms showing, was paddling the canoe as fast as he could paddle. Not quite that far, the pirogue was drifting.

Fargo had a choice to make. The Mad Indian or the pirogue. It was really no choice at all. Without the pirogue they were stranded. He set down the Henry, shucked the Colt and placed it next to the rifle, sat and tugged off his boots. By then the Mad Indian had vanished, but not the pirogue.

Trying not to think of gators and cottonmouths, Fargo waded in. It didn't help that he couldn't see under the surface. Anything could be down there.

The water rose to his knees. It rose to his waist. Kicking off, he swam after the pirogue. It was moving faster. A current had caught it.

Fargo pumped his arms and legs. He was a fair swimmer, but only fair. His skin never crawled as it was crawling now. He hated this, hated it with all he was.

To his left were floating plants he didn't know the name of. As he came up to them, they bulged upward. Something was underneath, and moving toward him.

Fargo wished he had the Colt. He wished it even more when an alligator's snout appeared. Then the eyes and the rest of the head. It was staring at him. He swam faster.

The short distance to the pirogue seemed like a mile.

Fargo glanced back just as the alligator sank under the water. Relief coursed through Fargo. He thought the gator had gone back under the plants. But no, a second later it reappeared, all of it this time, its tail flicking as it gave chase in an almost leisurely fashion.

It didn't matter that the gator wasn't much over five feet long. Its mouth was rimmed with the same sharp teeth as all other gators.

It could rip him open and take him under just as a bigger one would.

Fargo swam harder. Twenty feet to the pirogue, and the gator was more than halfway to him. He realized he wouldn't reach it in time. Stopping, he dog-paddled and brought his legs up to his chest. He had to pry at his pant leg to get hold of the Arkansas toothpick.

The alligator slowed and circled. Evidently it was unsure if he was suitable prey.

Fargo held the knife under the water and turned to keep the gator in front of him. He knew how fast they could strike. He also watched its tail. A blow from that could stun him and make him an easy meal.

The gator swam slowly.

Maybe it was only curious but Fargo couldn't count on that. From the island came yells. Remy and Namo were coming but they were a ways off yet.

"Fargo? Have you seen the Indian?"

"Why don't you answer?"

Fargo wanted to but it might provoke the alligator into attacking. The thing was beginning another circle. He continued to turn but his legs were growing tired. He couldn't tread water forever.

"Fargo? Where are you?"

Fargo took a gamble. They had rifles. They could scare the alligator off or send it to the bottom. "Here!" he hollered. "Come quick!"

The gator exploded into motion, coming at him with its mouth agape. Fargo kicked to one side and the jaws snapped shut inches from his chest. In an effort to keep them closed he grabbed at the snout and nearly lost his fingers. Swimming backward to put distance between them, he felt something bump his right leg. Something alive. Something that coiled around his leg as a snake would do. He glanced down but couldn't see what it was.

"Hell!"

A gator near him and a snake under him.

Fargo kicked but the snake—if it was one—clung on. And just then the alligator came at him, going for his neck and face. Which was exactly what Fargo wanted it to do. Twisting, he thrust up and in, sinking the toothpick to the hilt in the gator's throat.

In a twinkling the gator turned and swam for its plant sanctuary, the water growing bright with blood.

Fargo kicked at whatever was wrapped around his one leg and whatever it was slid off. He looked for the snake to rise up and bite him but nothing appeared. Not wasting another moment, he swam for the pirogue, which had lodged against a moss-encrusted cypress. He pulled himself up and over and lay on the bottom, grateful to be alive. A shaft of sunlight warmed his face but the rest of him was soaked. He slowly sat up and got hold of one of the paddles.

"Fargo? What on earth are you doing out there?"

"And where's the canoe?"

Remy and Namo were at the swamp's edge.

"Hold on," Fargo replied. He pushed free of the tree and made for the island. There was no sign of the alligator. Or of the Mad Indian, for that matter.

"You let him get away?" Namo said in reproach after Fargo had explained. "All we have done and we have nothing to show for it."

"He did what he could," Remy defended him. "Or did you miss the part about the alligator?"

Fargo was wiping the toothpick dry on grass. "I don't know about you two, but I don't intend to spend the rest of my life searching this godforsaken swamp. There's only one thing left for us to do."

Remy nodded. "We lure the razorback to us. Just as I have been saying we should do."

"We're not even sure it will work," Namo objected.

"There's plenty of wood on this island," Fargo noted. "We'll make a big fire, one that can be seen from a long ways off. The Mad Indian is bound to spot it. And with any luck, he'll set the boar on us."

"How do we kill it when it comes?" Namo asked.

"I have a plan," Skye Fargo said.

17

The sun had set an hour ago.

With the fading of the light and the advent of night, the creatures that liked the dark emerged and filled the air with their cries. Alligators bellowed. Frogs croaked. An occasional roar or shriek added to the din. The bleats and screams of prey told of predators hungry to fill their bellies.

On an island in the middle of that vast maze of water and violent life, Skye Fargo listened to the bedlam and was reminded of the Rockies. In the mountains, too, nighttime was when most of the meat-eaters were abroad. The yips of coyotes, the howls of wolves, the roars of bears and the screech of mountain lions—he looked forward to hearing them again, to being back in his element.

Here the bedlam was louder, and practically constant. Rare were the moments when the swamp fell still.

It was during one of those rare moments that Fargo heard a far-off squeal, and smiled. His shoulders were sore from all the digging they had done, but the work might prove worth it. From his hiding place in a thicket, he gazed out at the noisily crackling fire, and near it what appeared to be freshly overturned dirt.

"Pay us a visit, you bastard."

They were ready for the razorback, or as ready as they could hope to be. If it came, they stood a chance of ending the slaughter.

From where Fargo hunkered he couldn't see the others. Remy was under a tree. Namo was *in* one.

Fargo fingered the Sharps and shifted to relieve a cramp. It would be a long night if the razorback didn't show. He was glad his buckskins had finally dried. He'd had to sit uncomfortably close to the fire for half an hour.

Another squeal, closer than before.

Fargo munched on a piece of bread and imagined he was eating one of Liana's delicious meals. His stomach growled.

So did something else, from off in the brush.

Fargo tensed, then relaxed. Whatever it was, it wasn't the razorback. A cat of some kind, most likely a bobcat, and bobcats hardly ever attacked people. When they did, it was usually children. Fargo thought of Halette and Clovis, motherless. He thought of Pensee and Hetsutu.

"God, I hope you come."

Something rustled. A snake or some other small animal. Whatever it was moved away from him.

The wait wore on Fargo's nerves. The shadows seemed imbued with life. Leaves and branches moved but it was only the wind.

He heard no more squeals.

It was pushing midnight when a certain cry pricked Fargo's ears. He raised his head to hear better. It was repeated, not once but many times. The cry of a rabbit in distress.

The Mad Indian was luring the boar.

Fargo wondered if Remy and Namo had heard, and if they realized what the cries meant. He had half a mind to go warn them but they had agreed to stay where they were except for the few times Remy, who was nearest the fire, crept from concealment to add wood.

Remy would have to do so again soon. The flames were half as high as they had been.

A high-pitched screech pierced the gloom.

Fargo suspected that the rabbit had become food for the beast they were out to kill. He barely breathed and stayed perfectly still.

Then came another of those rare moments in which the great swamp fell quiet.

A log popped in the fire and smoke rose.

Fargo saw Remy come out from under the tree and move toward the fire. *Not now!* he wanted to shout. Hadn't Remy heard the rabbit?

Remy yawned and stepped to the pile of firewood they had gathered before the sun went down, enough to last the entire night. He added logs and stepped back as the flames brightened and flared.

Fargo moved toward the edge of the thicket. He must warn him to get back under cover.

That was when a huge shape materialized across the clearing. Two eyes gleamed balefully.

Remy didn't see it. He had his back to the shadow, which crept toward him on ghostly hooves.

Fargo jerked the Sharps up but didn't shoot. They needed the razorback to step on the circle of dirt.

Namo had seen the boar, too. And now he did what they had agreed not to do. "Remy! Behind you! *Le sanglier!*"

Remy whirled and brought up his rifle just as the razorback let out with a rumbling squeal and charged. Thinking fast, he sidestepped toward the dirt. The razorback was almost on top of him when he threw himself out of the way.

But he misjudged how ungodly quick the razorback could be.

The razorback and Remy seemed to merge. Remy went one way and the razorback went another. Remy to fly through the air and crash down on the upturned earth, the razorback to plow into the undergrowth.

"No!" Fargo hurtled from the thicket, firing as he unfurled a hasty shot that had no effect.

Namo banged off shots from up in the tree.

Fargo ran to the circle, and would never forget what awaited him.

They had done the best they could using branches and flat rocks to dig and scrape. The hole wasn't deep, only about four feet. A dozen sharp stakes were imbedded in the bottom. They had covered the pit with thin branches and grass and then spread dirt over the top.

"Dear God," Namo said at Fargo's side. "Is there no end to the horror?"

Remy had landed on his back. Two of the stakes had gone through his body, another through a leg, a third through an arm. He was still alive. He shook, and coughed, and spat up blood. And then he blinked up at them and said through his pain, "Tell me it is dead."

Fargo could hear splashing.

"It got away," Namo said.

"Damn. Then I die for nothing."

Namo dropped to a knee and reached down to touch Remy's shoulder. "We will get you out. It will take some doing but—"

"No."

"Non?"

Remy coughed and more blood oozed from the corners of his mouth. "I am done for, Namo. I know it and you know it." He sucked in a breath, and groaned. "Lord, the pain."

Namo appealed to Fargo. "We can't just let him die. We must do something. Help me."

"If we pull him off those stakes he won't live two minutes," Fargo predicted. Left down there, Remy might last five.

"We must try," Namo insisted. "You take his arms and I'll take his legs and we will slowly lift him out."

"He's in too much pain."

"I refuse to let him die this way. Do you hear me?"

Remy ended their argument by saying, "Shoot me."

Fargo and Namo looked at him and Namo said, "What?"

"You heard me. Shoot me. Put me out of misery. I am not long for this world anyway."

Now it was Namo who said, "No."

Remy tried to speak but what came out was more blood. His limbs convulsed, and he gasped out, "Don't let me suffer like this. I beg you."

Namo, averting his gaze, shook his head. "I can't. I just can't. I'm sorry. But I don't have it in me."

"I would do it for you."

"Don't say that." Namo wheeled and walked toward the fire, his chin on his chest.

Fargo knew what was coming.

"And you, monsieur? What about you? I have not known you long so it should be easier for you."

Fargo stared at the blood-wet stakes that stuck up out of Remy's body. More tremors wracked the Cajun, and he grit his teeth. "If I never see another swamp for as long as I live, it'll be too soon."

"Sorry?" Remy said, coughing. "What was that?"

"No one deserves to die like this."

Remy mustered a grin. "That is life, eh? None of us deserve the pain we bear but life doesn't care. It inflicts the pain anyway." He shook, then steadied, and wheezed, "Whenever you are ready."

Fargo placed his hand on his Colt.

"No!" Namo ran up and grabbed Fargo's wrist. "Don't do this! Life is too precious. Give him what few moments he has left."

Remy said, "Damn you, Namo. Leave the man alone." Then he did a strange thing—he laughed.

"Is your mind going?" Namo asked.

"It is the irony. I've never liked outsiders. Yet this man is an outsider and I like him. And now he is about to treat me with the mercy I have never shown others. Is that not ironic?"

"It is wrong."

"Let go of him, Namo."

"I refuse."

"In memory of Emmeline."

"Damn you, Remy. And damn the beast that did this to you." Namo forlornly stepped to one side.

"Such is life. We spend it holding the sadness at bay until the day when the final sadness comes over us." Remy had the worst coughing fit yet. "Just as it has come over me." He stared at Fargo. "Enough talk.

Do it. Get it over with. I don't know how much longer I can keep from screaming."

Fargo drew the Colt.

"Please," Namo said.

"Please," Remy echoed.

Fargo shot him square between the eyes. Hair, bone and brains rained on the bottom of the pit. Remy Cuvier went rigid, then limp. His eyes, locked open, were fixed on the stars.

"God in heaven," Namo said softly. "Is there no end?"

"Not until we're like him." Fargo nodded at the body.

"How can you be so callous? How can you be so cold? I thought you liked him."

"I did." Fargo replaced the spent cartridge, slid the Colt into his holster, and went over to the fire. He was suddenly bone tired. "I'll fix us some coffee."

"Now?" Namo said in amazement.

"We have to take turns keeping watch. I don't know about you but I can use some help staying awake."

"But after—" Namo said, and glanced at the pit. "It's just that my wife liked Romy. Of all her cousins, he was Emmeline's favorite. I could no more kill him than I could have killed her."

"There's no need to explain."

"Thank you. But what now? The boar escaped. Our trap failed, and cost us our friend. Do we go after it by ourselves or do we rethink how we should go about this?"

Fargo was opening a pack to get at the coffeepot. "I'm not giving up." Not this side of the grave he wasn't.

"And I am not suggesting we should," Namo set him straight. "But we have nothing to show for all our effort and sweat. The razorback is still out there. The Mad Indian, too."

"Those other men from Gros Ville are hunting them

too, remember?" Fargo reminded him. *"Maybe they'll have better luck than we have."*

"It is strange we haven't seen any sign of them."

"It's a big swamp."

"A huge swamp. But still, we should have run into them. Or seen their fires."

"Needles in a snake-infested haystack."

Namo commenced to pace. "Do you know what I think we should do?" He didn't wait for an answer. "We're not far from my cabin. I say we go there and rest a day or two. I will gather what news I can from my nearest neighbors, and we will plan and head out again."

As tired as Fargo was, he would rather keep at it, and said so.

"To what end?" Namo argued. "The beast is wise to us. Or if it isn't, the Mad Indian is."

Fargo recalled the rabbit cries.

"The pit trick won't work again. We must come up with something new. Something—what is the word?— foolproof."

From out in the swamp pealed a series of squeals, faint but unmistakable, punctuated by an all too human cackle.

"Do you hear?" Namo said. "They can go on as they are for years if they're not stopped. Think of the many innocents who will meet grisly ends."

"I'm here, aren't I?" Fargo reached into the pack and looked toward the pit. "Start covering that up."

"Oh. Oui. We can't let the wild things get at poor Remy." Namo went about halfway, and stopped. "What is this?" he said, stooping. "Bring a brand, if you would."

Blood speckled the ground. A lot of blood. The spots led toward where Remy had been standing when the boar rammed into him, and then off into the undergrowth.

"One of us hit it!" Namo exclaimed.

Fargo suspected it was his shot.

"Wouldn't it be wonderful if it proves fatal? Let

the beast suffer as poor Remy suffered. Let it die a lingering death."

As if to mock them, the night was shattered by shrieks.

Human shrieks.

18

The swamp at night was ten times as dangerous as during the day.

Ten times darker, too.

Fargo was in the bow, Namo in the stern. The cypress grove they were gliding through was thick with moss and silence. The living things had gone quiet, with one exception. It was the exception that brought them here, the exception that raised the hackles on their necks.

The shrieks had faded a long time ago. They thought that was the end of it, that whoever had been shrieking was dead.

Then the other cries started. Wails and screams and what sounded like blubbering. The cries went on and on until Fargo and Namo couldn't take hearing them, until they had to come see who it was that was suffering the torment of the damned.

They had finished covering Remy, thrown the pack into the pirogue, and here they were. The cool night air added to the bumps that crawled up and down their skin.

Fargo had lost count of how many times he thought he saw something moving, only it turned out to be moss or a tree or nothing at all but his imagination.

"Why is it so quiet all of a sudden?" Namo Heuse whispered. "Do you think the man is dead?"

"I don't know." Fargo's instincts warned him the razorback must be near.

Suddenly new cries reached them.

"Listen!" Namo exclaimed. "It curdles my blood."

The cries would curdle anyone's. The man was wailing and blubbering and mouthing incoherent words. He couldn't be far, maybe a hundred yards ahead.

Fargo slowed and whispered for Namo to do the same.

There was a splash to their right. A single splash, and whatever made it was gone.

Gradually a spit of land took vague shape. Off in the vegetation a finger of orange appeared.

"A fire!" Namo whispered.

"I have eyes."

"You will think I am crazy but I think I know that voice. His name is Toussaint. He is from Gros Ville."

"One of the men hunting the razorback?"

"Oui."

They coasted the last twenty feet. A small cove spread open. Already grounded was another pirogue. They brought their pirogue to a stop next to it and quickly climbed out. Then, rifles at the ready, they moved forward.

Fargo was in the lead. He tried to avoid stepping on twigs or dry growth that crunched underfoot but in the pitch black it was hard to do. He mentally swore each time he made unwanted noise. The only consolation was that Namo made more.

The scent of smoke was strong. As they neared the fire it was mixed with the smell of something else—fresh blood.

Fargo had smelled blood too many times not to know what it was.

The growth was ungodly thick. Try as they might, they couldn't spot the man who kept crying out.

A new sound reached them, and brought them to a stop.

A low, insane cackle.

"The Mad Indian!" Namo breathed.

Fargo bent and peered through the tangle but all he saw was the campfire.

"What can that fiend be doing?"

"We'll soon find out." Fargo went even more slowly.

133

They had a chance here to put an end to the lunatic and he wouldn't squander it.

"We can't let him get away," Namo gave voice to the same thought.

"Hush."

They became two snails, creeping along. A clearing appeared. At the center, the fire. Nearby lay a body. The chest had been torn wide, exposing shattered ribs and internal organs. The razorback's handiwork.

Another Cajun was spread eagle, staked out at the wrists and ankles, and as naked as the day he was born. He writhed and whimpered and blubbered, sounding almost as mad as the person bent over him.

The Mad Indian was holding a knife. Drops of blood dripped from the tip. Tittering, he grinned down at Toussaint and held out something the size of an olive that appeared to be dangling from the end of a string.

Fargo's stomach churned. That olive was one of Toussaint's eyes. The Mad Indian had dug it out with his knife.

"Whimper, whimper, white dog. Sing your song of pain."

Toussaint whimpered.

"Now scream for me, white cur. Scream so the frogs can hear." The Mad Indian slashed off a chunk of flesh.

Toussaint screamed.

"So happy you make me," the Mad Indian said gleefully. "I hate your kind. Hate, hate, hate."

Namo slid up next to Fargo. "We'll fire at the same time. One of us is bound to hit him."

Suddenly the Mad Indian glanced up, straight at them. He cocked his head, his eyes glittering like sparks.

"How can he have heard me?" Namo whispered.

Fargo raised the Sharps. Or tried to. The heavy

growth that hemmed them made it next to impossible to bring it to his shoulder.

"What have we here?" the Mad Indian said, and laughed his demented laugh. "More rabbits, I fear." Suddenly he spun and bounded for the far side of the clearing.

"No!" Namo yelled, and snapped off a shot.

Fargo got the Sharps up and took aim but the Mad Indian was weaving erratically. He curled his finger to the trigger just as the spindly figure vanished into the vegetation.

"Damn it."

They forced their way to the clearing.

Namo paused next to the dead man to say sorrowfully, "I know this one, too. He has a wife and three small children. Or had, I should say. They will take the news hard."

Fargo was trying to look at Toussaint and keep the contents of his stomach down. The things the Mad Indian had done would make an Apache envious. Hideous, despicable things no one could endure without breaking.

Toussaint's good eye was open and had a wild light in it that wasn't much different from the wild light in the eyes of the Mad Indian.

"Dear God, no," Namo said.

Fargo drew his Colt.

"Wait!" Namo squatted and put a hand on the other's chest. "Toussaint, can you hear me? It is I, Namo."

The man blubbered.

"Your name is Henri Toussaint. Remember? Think of who you are and where you are."

Toussaint let out a loud sob.

"Is there anything you want me to tell your woman and your children? Any last words?"

Again Toussaint sobbed, only softer.

"Can you hear me? Both your ears are gone but you should still be able to hear. Talk to me, Henri. Say something."

Incredibly, the ruin did. "Namo?"

"*Oui*. The Mad Indian has run off. But I swear to you by all that is holy, he will pay for his deeds."

Toussaint's throat, what was left of it, bobbed. "The boar . . . it came at us so fast . . . no warning. It got Philippe. Ripped him open."

"I know. I will bury him."

"It . . . rushed me . . . knocked me out. When I woke . . . my clothes were gone . . . I was staked . . . the Mad Indian . . ."

"Enough about him. What do I say to your wife? What do I say to your children?"

Toussaint took a deep breath. "What else? Tell them I love them. Tell them I am sorry."

"For what?"

Fargo said, "What about the other men from Gros Ville? Where did they get to?"

"Who was that?"

"It is the outsider, the scout I sent for," Namo explained. "And my friend," he added.

Again the stricken man had to take a deep breath before he could say, "We separated . . . maybe razorback got them, too."

"You should have stayed together. There is strength in numbers."

"We thought . . . cover more area." Toussaint stopped and went to lick his lips only there were no lips to lick. "Oh, God. What has that lunatic done to me? I am not long for this world."

"I can put you out of your misery if you want," Fargo offered.

"*Non. Merci*. But it will . . . not be long. Life is precious. So very precious. We do not . . . do not appre . . ."

"Don't talk so much," Namo said. "Conserve your strength. Would you like some water? I will gladly give you some. Henri? Can you hear me?" He bent low, his ear over the other's travesty of a mouth. "He's not breathing."

Fargo sighed. One by one they were being wiped

out. Although the Cajuns liked to call the swamp their home, it was the razorback, and the Mad Indian, who were most at home here. Pit civilized men against a beast in the wild and the beast would win nearly every time.

Namo sat back, dejected. "Is there no end? How many more must die before we end this nightmare?"

"We should bury them so we can turn in," Fargo said tiredly.

"Very well." Namo rose and took a step toward the trees. "I'll find something to dig with."

They both heard the *twang*.

"Get down!" Fargo yelled, and dived.

Namo was too slow. The arrow caught him in the thigh and twisted him half-around. Gritting his teeth, he pitched flat and fired a wild shot into the undergrowth.

A crazed cackle told them he missed.

Fargo palmed his Colt. He expected more arrows but instead heard crackling and crashing. The Mad Indian was fleeing. Leaving the Sharps there, he pumped his legs. Namo shouted for him to stop. Limbs tore at his buckskins. A branch scratched his cheek.

A figure took shape, the Mad Indian bounding like one of the rabbits he used to lure the razorback. A pale face glanced back at him and another cackle tickled the air.

Fargo snapped off a shot, knowing he had missed even as he squeezed the trigger. He was too eager.

A low limb caught him, sending ripples of pain across his shoulders. He kept running. He began to gain.

The Mad Indian looked back again and this time he didn't laugh. He redoubled his effort.

Fargo yearned for a clear shot. Just one. He thought he had it and snapped the Colt up but more growth got in the way. He ran. He ran and he ran. And he tripped. An exposed root caught him about the ankle and the next thing he knew he was flat on his face.

The lunatic tittered.

"Not this time," Fargo vowed. He heaved erect.

The Mad Indian was nowhere to be seen.

Splashing suggested why. Fargo vaulted a log and burst through high grass and had to dig in his heels to keep from barreling into the water.

The canoe was a blot in the dark, the Indian paddling furiously. "Mad, mad, mad, mad, mad!"

Fargo extended his arm and did something he had rarely ever done—he shot a man in the back.

The Mad Indian stiffened, and howled. But he didn't stop paddling and in another heartbeat the night enveloped him like a shroud.

"Son of a bitch." Fargo was beginning to think that if it wasn't for bad luck, he wouldn't have any luck at all. He lingered, hoping the Mad Indian would reappear, but then he thought of Namo and hastened in disgust back to the clearing.

Namo was by the fire, trying in vain to get the arrow out. Beads of sweat speckled his face as he grunted and said, "I'm glad you're back. I can't do this myself."

Fargo knelt. The shaft had gone all the way through and the barbed tip was protruding from the back of the thigh.

"I heard a shot. Did you get him?"

"I hit him but he got away."

"Remy was right. God is on the Indian's side."

"Don't talk nonsense."

"Where did he get the bow? I didn't see a bow when he was bent over Toussaint. Did you see a bow?"

"He must have had it in the trees." Fargo examined the barbed tip. It was made from bone and slick with wet blood. He moved so the firelight played over it, and frowned.

"What is the matter?"

"How do you feel?"

"How do you think I feel?" Namo snapped, then closed his eyes and said, "Sorry. I am weak from the blood I have lost. And cold. Very cold. It came over me suddenly." He shuddered, and bit his lower lip. "Why do you ask?"

"There's something else on the tip of this arrow besides blood."

"What?"

"Poison."

19

Fargo stroked strongly, smoothly, and tried not to think of the man lying in the bottom of the pirogue. It was a race against time and time was winning.

The Atchafalaya during the day was so different from the Atchafalaya at night. They were two worlds. The patches of sunlight, the chirps and warbles of the day birds, the butterflies, made the swamp seem more hospitable. Not that Fargo relaxed his guard. Under that friendlier surface lurked the same menaces.

"How much longer?" Fargo asked. When Heuse didn't answer, he asked louder. "How much longer, Namo?"

The Cajun rose on an elbow and gazed over the gunwale. He was sickly pale and slick with sweat. "Another hour, maybe less. Keep going as you are."

"What's the next landmark?"

"You will come to a bayou. Follow it south."

Fargo grunted. They would make better time in a bayou. And he much preferred the more open water to the gloom and mire of the swamp. "Lie back down and rest. I'll get us to your cabin. Don't you worry."

"I am past worrying. Now I think only of staying alive."

They intended to rest at the cabin a short while and then push on to the settlement where there was a healer Namo knew. Not a doctor in the normal sense but a woman versed in herbs and medicinal lore. Namo believed she might be able to counter the effect of the Mad Indian's poison.

Fargo hoped so. So far Namo was holding his own but bit by bit the toxin, whatever it was, was sapping Namo's vitality. Fargo wondered if the Mad Indian picked a slow-acting poison on purpose so his victims suffered more. It sounded like something the lunatic would do.

Ever since setting out he'd had the feeling they were being followed but he never once saw anyone. It could be nerves. The swamp, the violence, the dying, had gotten to him.

Fargo never knew but when the razorback would hurtle out of the shadows. It preyed on him the worst of anything, making him jumpy, making him see things that weren't there.

"I'm turning into a little girl," Fargo said in disgust. It made him think of Halette.

"What was that, *mon ami*?"

"Nothing. I was talking to myself."

"I'm sorry I am not better company."

"You should sleep."

"I pass out and wake up and pass out again. One minute my blood is on fire, the next it is ice. And my lungs aren't working as they should. Sometimes I find it hard to breathe."

Fargo clenched his jaw. Damn the Mad Indian to hell.

Namo chuckled, but it came out like dry seeds rattling in a gourd. "In a way I should be thankful."

"For what?" Fargo asked. The man had lost his wife and friends and now was dying himself.

"That the poison works so slowly. The Mad Indian could have used one that kills instantly."

"Not that vengeful bastard."

Slowly sitting up so his back was propped against the side, Namo licked his bluish lips. "We can't blame him, you know."

"Sure we can. He shot the arrow. He put the poison on the tip."

"No. Not that. I mean we can't blame him for hating us. For hating all whites over the deaths of his people. He's the last of his kind. That is bound to have affected his mind."

Fargo thought of the Mandans, a once powerful tribe on the upper Missouri, nearly wiped out by smallpox. He thought of other tribes, decimated by white disease. It was never the other way around. Whites always introduced disease to the Indians. The Indians never introduced disease to the whites. Until the whites came along, many tribes had been largely disease-free.

"I hate him for killing my wife," Namo was saying, "but not for this." He touched his leg. "I understand why he hates so much. Were I in his moccasins, I would hate us too."

"Hate doesn't excuse it. And you're forgetting the razorback."

"Forget the beast that tore apart my Emmeline? Never." Namo coughed, and covered his mouth with his hand. When he lowered it his fingers and palm were flecked with scarlet. "But you must admit it is brilliant of him, *non*?"

"You're delirious. It's the fever."

"I'm not out of my mind yet," Namo assured him. "And it is brilliant. When did you ever hear of anyone using a razorback to kill his enemies? If that is not brilliant, I don't know what is."

"If you're not delirious you're close to it."

Namo smiled. "Very well. Have it your way. But we Cajuns do not think less of our enemies simply because they *are* our enemies. We can respect them when they deserve it."

"The only thing the Mad Indian deserves is lead between the eyes."

"You can be quite vicious. Do you know that?"

"That's your word," Fargo said. And since the talk seemed to be helping take Namo's mind off his pain, he added, "Look. I'm not big on forgive and forget. I don't turn the other cheek. Hit me and I'll knock your damn teeth out. Try to stab me in the back and

I'll blow out your wick. If you want to call that vicious, go ahead. Me, I call it practical."

"What about mercy, monsieur? Where does that enter in?"

"Depends on the time and the place and if the person deserves it."

"You are judge, jury and hangman? Is that how it goes."

"When I have to be." Fargo glanced behind them. "On the frontier there's not much law. Hell, in some places there isn't any. Some parts of the Rockies haven't even been explored yet. A man is on his own. He's his own law."

"I don't know if I would like your mountains very much. I like the peace of the swamp."

Fargo almost laughed. "If you call this peace I'd hate to see what you call trouble."

Namo made that dry gourd sound. "I am used to the alligators and the cottonmouths. Just as you are to the big bears and the big cats where you come from."

"I may see a bear or a mountain lion once a month," Fargo said. "I've lost count of the alligators and snakes I've seen here."

"Fleas are fleas, whether many or small."

Now Fargo did laugh. The notion of calling a thousand-pound grizzly a flea struck his funny bone. "You're a strange hombre, Cajun."

"Thank you. I take that as a compliment. The truth is, we Cajuns think you outsiders are strange."

"It never occurred to any of you that living in a gator- and snake-infested swamp is a mite peculiar?"

Now it was Namo who laughed but his laughter changed to hacking coughs and he doubled over. His whole body shook, and he groaned. When the fit subsided, he looked up, his mouth rimmed with red. "I'm afraid I am going to pass out again." And he did.

Fargo swore and stopped paddling. He placed a hand to the Cajun's forehead. It was on fire. He checked Namo's pulse. It was terribly weak, barely a flutter.

Fargo bent to the paddle anew. Now and then he checked over his shoulder. Along about the ninth or tenth time he glanced back, far off in the gloomy cypress, well out of rifle range, he caught movement. He saw it for only a few seconds but that was enough.

It was a canoe.

The Mad Indian must have followed them all night.

Fargo was tempted to stop and lie in ambush but he had Namo to think of. Namo's chances were slim as it was. Any delay in reaching the healer would seal his fate.

His shoulders were sore and his arms ached but Fargo ignored them. He glanced back often but didn't spot the Indian a second time. The wily madman wouldn't make the same mistake twice.

Presently Fargo came to the bayou. He turned to the south as Namo had instructed. A pair of cranes took wing. A bullfrog croaked and leaped from a log.

Here was Fargo's chance to put more distance between him and his insane shadow. His body protested but he stroked with renewed purpose, the pirogue cleaving the surface like a knife. Namo hadn't said how far the cabin was. Or, for that matter, whether it was right on the bayou or hidden somewhere.

The sun was low in the sky. Fargo hoped to reach the cabin before dark. He figured to rest a couple of hours and then push on. No more than that. Namo needed the healer too badly.

The breeze picked up. To the west a bank of low clouds formed.

Fargo frowned. This was all he needed. Rain, on top of everything else.

The bayou neared an island. Fargo was staring into the distance, seeking sign of the cabin. He almost missed the narrow wooden landing. A path led toward tall willows and the squat square bulk of a log cabin.

Fargo let out a whoop. He brought the pirogue in next to the landing and tied it to a cleat. Then, bending over Namo, he shook him and said his name a few times.

The Cajun was slow to stir. He blinked, and licked his lips. "*Le peau me cuit. Avez-vous quelque chose de calmant?*"

"I didn't get any of that," Fargo said.

"Eh? Oh. *Pardon*. What is it? What's wrong?"

"We're here."

"Where?"

Fargo put a hand to Namo's brow. It was hotter than ever. "At your cabin. I'm going to carry you inside."

"*Bêtise*."

"What?"

"Nonsense. I will walk."

"In the shape you're in?" Fargo reached for him but the Cajun shrugged him off and slowly sat up. "Don't be so stubborn."

"I have my dignity." Namo groped and braced both hands and managed to get to his knees. "Be patient. It takes a lot out of me."

"We don't have all night. There's a storm coming in." Fargo grabbed the Sharps and Namo's rifle and climbed onto the landing. "I'll put these in your cabin and be right back." It would free his hands to carry him.

"There is no hurry. I am doing this myself."

Fargo shook his head and jogged up the path. The cabin was sturdily built, pride of craft evident in the fit of the logs and the caulking. He tried the latch and the door swung in on leather hinges. The room was nicely furnished, including a bearskin rug in front of a stone fireplace. Two doorways opened into bedrooms, one with bunk beds for the children and a larger room for the parents. Fargo set the rifles on a table and hastened back down.

Namo had managed to climb out of the pirogue and was on his side, breathing raggedly, his chest heaving. "I need to rest a bit."

"We don't have time for this." Fargo slipped one arm under the Cajun's legs and the other under his shoulders.

"I can do it, I tell you," Namo weakly protested. "Put me down."

Paying no heed, Fargo took him to the cabin. "I'll put you in bed and make something for you to eat."

"I'm not helpless. The rocking chair will do fine."

The rocking chair it was.

Fargo found a blanket and covered him to the chin. "You're trembling. If you have the chills I can get a fire going."

"I'm hot and cold both. What kind of poison did he use, do you think? Snake venom?"

"We would have to ask him and he'd never tell."

"I have heard that one tribe rubs the tips of their arrows over a certain kind of toad." Namo coughed, then said, "That food you mentioned sounds nice. I am famished."

The cupboard was full. In a pantry were dried venison and carrots and potatoes. Fargo decided to make soup. He kindled a fire in the fireplace, then took a bucket from the counter and headed down to the bayou for water.

Dark clouds now covered most of the sky and to the west bright flashes were punctuated by distant rumbles.

Fargo filled the bucket and started back up. He heard a splash but concentric ripples suggested a fish was to blame.

Namo had passed out again.

Fargo poured water into a black cook pot and hung the cook pot in the fireplace. He chopped carrots and potatoes and sliced the venison and dropped them in.

The rest of the water went into a coffeepot. Fargo needed that more than food. He was exhausted.

Outside, the wind keened. A branch thwacked the roof. Thunder rumbled ever louder.

Namo tossed and turned in the chair, frequently mumbling in fever-induced delirium.

Pattering drew Fargo over to the window. The Heusees had gone to the expense of installing a glass pane. He moved the curtain aside and peered out. Heavy drops were falling. Down at the landing the pirogue bobbed up and down in the wind-driven swell.

There was no sign of the Mad Indian.

Fargo reckoned it would be a while yet.

Then a lightning bolt seared the heavens and the bolt's flash bathed the cabin and the willows, revealing a scarecrow figure a stone's throw from the window.

Revealed him so clearly, Fargo could see the scarecrow's mad grin.

20

Fargo drew his Colt and started to turn toward the door, but just like that the Mad Indian was gone, melted into the willows like the ghost some thought him to be.

Lowering the curtains, Fargo went to the door anyway. Instead of going out, he lifted a heavy bar propped against the wall and slid it into the two slots on the back of the door, then gave the bar a shake. It would take a battering ram to get through—or a razorback as big as a buffalo.

Namo had slumped in his chair and the blanket had fallen off. Fargo pressed a palm to the Cajun's forehead and it was the same as before—burning hot. Since Namo was out to the world, he couldn't object to Fargo carrying him to the bedroom and putting him on the big bed. There were no windows, only the thick walls. Fargo covered him and went out.

The storm had broken in all its elemental fury.

Cradling the Sharps, Fargo took up his position at the window. Large drops splashed the pane in a liquid deluge. The wind howled, bending the trees as if they were so many blades of grass. The glimpse he had of the bayou showed it being frothed into a fury.

Would the razorback be out on a night like this? Fargo wondered. Or would it do as most animals did and seek cover?

The blaze of bolts and the crash of thunder were continuous. Fargo hadn't seen a storm this violent since he left the mountains. Some of the lightning was so close, the thunder shook the cabin.

And somewhere in that tempest, plotting to kill them, was the Mad Indian.

Fargo was glad there was only the one window and door. He was also glad about the rain. For as long as it lasted, and until the logs dried, the Mad Indian couldn't set the cabin on fire.

The chirp of the coffeepot brought Fargo to the fireplace. The coffee was ready, the stew was piping hot. He found bowls in the cupboard and a wooden ladle to fill them with, and spoons. He took one of the bowls to the bedroom and sat on the edge of the bed.

"Namo?"

Heuse didn't stir.

"Namo?" Fargo was averse to waking him but the man needed nourishment. He shook Namo's shoulder a few times. "Time to eat."

Eyelids fluttering, Namo Heuse rolled onto his back and slowly sat up, his head and shoulders propped against the headboard. "How long was I out?"

"A while."

More thunder shook the cabin to its foundation. Namo glanced sharply at the ceiling. "I seem to remember you saying something about a storm."

Fargo dipped the spoon in the soup. "Open up."

"I will feed myself, thank you very much."

Fargo placed the bowl in Namo's lap and gave him the spoon. "If you were any more pigheaded, you'd be a razorback."

Namo dipped the spoon and raised it to his mouth, his teeth gritting with the effort.

"There's plenty more where this came from so if you want seconds give me a holler."

"I can't tell you how good it is. I'm starved."

"It will help with the fever." Fargo stood. "If you're sure that you can do it yourself—?"

"I am. Thank you." Namo let him get as far as the doorway before asking, "Is something the matter?"

"No."

"Is it the Mad Indian? Did he come after us?"

Fargo grimly nodded.

"I expected as much. We have been a thorn in his side. He wants us dead more than anyone. This is good."

"You think so?"

"We can end this once and for all. As soon as I gather my strength, I will be out to help you."

"You get out of that bed and I'll throw you back in again," Fargo promised. "Leave everything to me." He made it a point to close the bedroom door behind him.

Fargo added a log to the fire. He filled a bowl with soup and went to the window. It didn't look as if the storm would end any time soon. Fine by him. It bought them time to rest, to recuperate. The soup made him drowsy so he filled a cup with bubbling coffee. It wasn't enough. He drank two more.

Fargo didn't like being cooped up. He prowled the room like a caged panther. Once he thought he heard a thump against the side of the cabin. It wasn't repeated, and he figured a tree limb was to blame.

Namo called out that he was done so Fargo went in. He offered to bring a second bowl but the Cajun declined.

"It might make me sick. I need sleep more than anything. As it is, I can't hold my head up."

"Then don't." Fargo backed out. "If you need anything, anything at all, give a holler."

"You will make some woman a fine husband one day."

"Go to hell."

Namo chuckled.

The storm was finally slackening. The lightning strikes were fewer and the boom of thunder less.

Fargo looked out the window. As best he could tell, by some miracle the pirogue was still tied to the landing. On an impulse he went to the door, removed the bar, and opened it. Drops wet his face. Wind fanned his cheeks. Everything was drenched—the ground, the thickets, the trees.

Silhouetted as he was in the doorway, Fargo only

stood there a few seconds. Just long enough to scan the vicinity. Then he stepped back and started to close the door.

That was when he heard it, from out of the willows, the bleat of a small animal. A bleat he had heard on several occasions now. The bleat of a rabbit tied to a stake.

Fargo slammed the door and replaced the bar. It wouldn't be long. He took to pacing until he noticed an axe in the corner. He placed it on the table. He added a butcher knife and a meat cleaver. Casting about for more weapons, his gaze alighted on the wood bin. Several of the logs were thin enough that they sparked an idea. He selected three, sat at the chair and used the butcher knife to whittle. When he had three sharp points, he placed them next to the axe.

Was there anything else he could use? A lantern suggested an idea. He lit it and turned the wick low and placed the lantern in the middle of the table, not for the extra light but as a possible weapon.

There was nothing else, not unless Fargo counted table knives in a drawer, and a broom.

The cries of the rabbit seemed louder.

The rain had stopped and the wind had died.

Fargo went to the window. Remembering the Mad Indian's bow, he was careful not to show himself. The night was still and silent save for the bait. He was about to turn away when another cry, from out of the dark heart of the swamp, caused his pulse to quicken.

The razorback had heard the rabbit.

It was on its way.

Fargo tried to swallow in a mouth gone suddenly dry. He crossed to the bedroom. Namo was sound asleep. Loathe to disturb him, Fargo closed the bedroom door. The cabin walls were thick enough that Namo should be safe. Not even the boar could break them down. Still, on second thought, Fargo left the door open a crack.

A squeal sounded uncomfortably near.

Fargo hefted the Sharps and moved to the window. It was the weak spot, the cabin's Achilles heel. Would the razorback sense that? He backed up until he bumped against the table. It would be soon. He could feel it in his bones. He heard a cackle, and the loudest squeal yet.

The side of the cabin was struck a resounding blow. Dust particles gleamed, sifting slowly to the floor.

Fargo wedged the heavy Sharps to his shoulder and thumbed back the hammer. More blows thudded, each closer to the window than the last. The razorback squealed in baffled rage. It wanted in but Namo had built too well. The walls were too sturdy.

Suddenly its porcine face filled the window, its tusks curved like twin sabers. Its dark eyes glowed red.

Fargo knew it saw him. He fired and the glass pane dissolved in a shower of shards. Blood spurted, and in a twinkling the boar was gone, squealing and screeching.

Fargo fed in a new cartridge and set himself. "Don't keep me waiting, you bastard."

It didn't.

With an ear-splitting squeal the razorback slammed into the window. What was left of the glass showered down and the frame buckled. Fargo fired, reloaded, raised the rifle to fire again.

The boar was stuck! Its head was wedged fast.

Fargo squeezed off another shot. He should have killed it; he had the thing dead to rights. But the razorback, in its wild thrashing, moved its head just as he fired and the slug intended for the creature's brainpan cored a shoulder instead. The razorback was beside itself. Wood cracked and splintered as the window gave way. But the opening still wasn't wide enough. The razorback couldn't get inside. Squealing in frustration, it bounded into the night.

Fargo girded for the next onslaught. He stayed focused on the window. That was the only reason he caught the blur of motion and sprang aside with a hair to spare. A feather shaft imbedded itself next to the fireplace, quivering.

The Mad Indian cackled.

Fargo had to remember he was up against two adversaries, not just one. He squatted, hoping the crazed warrior would show himself.

There was another thud. The front wall, this time. Twice more the razorback slammed into the cabin. And then the inevitable happened—the boar rammed into the door. The bar held but the jamb cracked. The beast struck the door again, nearly tearing it off its hinges.

The heavy bar held but it wouldn't for long. Fargo trained the Sharps on the center of the door. Out of the corner of his eye he watched the window, too, and when a thin figure filled it, an arrow notched to a sinew string, he threw himself flat. The string twanged and the shaft whizzed over his head.

Simultaneously, the living engine of destruction attacked the door. Again the bar held but cracks appeared.

The Mad Indian sprang out of sight.

Fargo swung the Sharps from the door to the window and back again. Hooves drummed, and the door burst as the window had done, bits and slivers flying. Part of the bar flew past Fargo's head. He took swift aim and fired.

The razorback was framed in the opening. At the shot, its dark eyes locked on Fargo and it hurtled toward him, squealing and tucking its chin to rake with its tusks. Fargo threw himself to the right and the boar pounded past. He inadvertently put his back to the window, and a chill rippled down his spine at a cackle from the Mad Indian.

Fargo didn't look; he scrambled toward the table. An arrow with a discolored bone tip thunked into the floorboards inches from his arm.

Letting go of the Sharps, Fargo rolled, palming the Colt as he turned. The Mad Indian was at the window, nocking another arrow. Flat on his back, Fargo fanned off two swift shots and was rewarded with a yelp. The Mad Indian disappeared.

Across the room, the razorback had wheeled to come at him again but its hooves were finding slick purchase on the smooth boards.

Fargo fanned two shots so quickly they sounded as one. Then he was under the table and the boar was pounding past but as it went by it hooked the table with a tusk and upended it. Fargo felt a pain across his shoulders. The table had landed on top of him. Shoving it off, he gained his knees. The axe was only a few feet away. He grabbed it up, and stood.

The razorback came at him yet again, squealing, its beady eyes ablaze. Its tusks swept up and in.

Fargo sidestepped. He put all he had into swinging the axe and the edge bit deep into the razorback's neck. He tried to jerk it free but the handle was torn from his grasp.

Once more the boar wheeled. It paused, wheezing, blood misting from the new wound.

At Fargo's feet lay the meat cleaver and one of the logs he had sharpened. He scooped them up.

The razorback stood there, glaring. In the confines of the cabin it seemed enormous beyond belief.

The boar tensed to spring forward.

And that was when the bedroom door opened. Namo Heuse, caked in sweat, blanket over his shoulders, blinked and said in dazed confusion, "Fargo? I thought I heard a noise."

The razorback spun.

And Fargo flew, taking the gamble of his life. He stabbed the stake into the razorback's eye. Out of instinct the razorback jerked away, and collided with the wall. It stumbled, then righted itself just as Fargo brought the meat cleaver down. Again and again and again Fargo swung. His life was in the balance.

The terror of the Atchafalaya squealed. With the axe sticking from its neck and the stake jutting from its eyes, it took a step toward him—and died. The crash of its great body rattled dishes in the cupboard.

"You did it!" Namo marveled.

Fargo dashed to the Sharps. Reloading on the fly, he raced out the front door and around the corner. But he needn't have worried.

The stick figure in the mud was as still as death could make it, the eyes, even in oblivion, twin mirrors of madness.

Namo appeared at the window. "Is he—?"

"He is."

"Then it's over? It's really and truly over?"

"Except for getting you to the healer in the settlement." Suddenly so weary he could barely stand, Fargo leaned against the cabin.

"There's no rush, my friend. The meal and the rest did wonders. I think my fever broke. We can wait until daylight."

Fargo smiled for the first time in days. "I can use some rest myself. And something more to eat."

Namo Heuse glanced over his shoulder. "How would you like roast boar?"

LOOKING FORWARD!
The following is the opening
section from the next novel in the exciting
Trailsman series from Signet:

**THE TRAILSMAN #330
TUCSON TYRANT**

*Tucson, Arizona Territory, 1860—
where "stranglers" rule supreme and a
beautiful woman's embrace is the dance
of death.*

The sound of gunfire ripped through the furnace-hot desert air, but the lone, crop-bearded rider astride a black-and-white pinto stallion ignored it. One or two shots, the rider mused idly, usually meant celebration fire, just drunks hurrahing the town. Three or more often meant somebody was six feet closer to hell.

"Time to tank up, old campaigner," Skye Fargo told the stallion, reining in at a small spring just outside the siesta-prone, but dangerous, settlement of Tucson in south-central Arizona Territory.

Fargo had been feeling a case of the nervous fantods for the past twenty miles or so. With the bluecoat pony soldiers being pulled from nearby Camp Grant for the rumored war brewing back east, three dangerous tribes—Comanche, Kiowa, and Apache—were making life hell for everyone else out here.

Fargo dipped his dusty head into the cool spring water, then cupped handfuls and drank them. Next he dropped the Ovaro's bridle and let him drink. More gunfire erupted from town, and Fargo thumbed back the rawhide riding thong from the hammer of his single-action Colt.

"Don't go looking for your own grave," he muttered, advice from a Ute warrior, up in the Mormon country, just before the Ute almost killed him. But when had the Trailsman, as some called Fargo, ever done the *safe* thing?

Fargo studied Tucson and the surrounding terrain from slitted eyes. He was a tall, rangy, sinew-tough man wearing buckskins and a wide-brimmed plainsman's hat. His face was tanned hickory nut brown above the darker brown of his beard. Eyes the pure blue of a mountain lake stayed in constant motion.

Fargo didn't like what he was seeing—and not seeing. In places sagebrush grew tall enough to hide a man, and as Fargo had ridden across the dreaded desert of southern Arizona Territory in the past few days, he had spotted rock mounds where victims of Indian attack had been buried—killed by Apaches, most likely.

But the view within the town limits was just as ominous. At first glance, all Fargo could see through blurry heat waves was the steeple of a massive San Antonio church at the head of the central plaza. A green expanse of barley land ringed the town, cultivation meeting the desert like a knife edge. Strips of cottonwood lined the little Santa Cruz River, which divided the narrow and fertile valley where the mining-supply center of Tucson was located.

None of that, however, impressed Fargo as much as the slumping body hanging from a cottonwood limb near the river. He couldn't read the sign pinned to it, so he retrieved his brass binoculars from a saddle pocket.

" 'Jerked to Jesus,' " he read aloud, shaking his head in disgust.

There were no Rangers out here as had recently been formed in Texas, and not enough marshals to fill an outhouse. Fargo had been warned, before he left Fort Yuma, about Tucson's notorious Committee for Public Safety. Furthermore, he vastly preferred the Arizona Territory as it looked farther north, a mostly unpopulated landscape of pine trees, granite cliffs, and air that didn't cling in your lungs like molten glass.

But Fargo was a victim of events. He had recently lost a high-stakes match against a pretty redhead who ran a faro wheel, and a sorely needed job as a fast-messenger rider awaited him here.

Fargo snugged the bridle again, the Ovaro taking the bit easily, and swung up into leather. He took a moment to slide his sixteen-shot Henry rifle from its saddle scabbard and check the vulnerable tube magazine for dents. Then he spurred the Ovaro forward, aiming for the central plaza at the heart of town.

Not much had changed, Fargo quickly realized, since last time he'd ridden these unpaved, sun-drenched streets. Lumber was scarce in the region, and most of the buildings were of Indian-style puddled adobe with brush ramadas shading the doors. Not one hotel or store, but plenty of twenty-four-hour gambling houses. Fargo heard lilting Spanish everywhere. The place was still overrun with dogs, whose constant yapping made the Ovaro stutter-step nervously.

When Fargo's eyes flicked to the rammed-earth sidewalks, the two-legged curs watching him from hooded glances bothered him even more. The local vigilantes were as obvious as bedbugs on a clean sheet, for they all carried double-ten scatterguns, barrels sawed off to ten inches.

"Mr. Fargo? Mr. Skye Fargo?"

Excerpt from *TUCSON TYRANT*

At the sound of a musical female voice, Fargo tugged rein and slued around in the saddle. A young woman stood in the doorway of a two-story adobe house that fronted on the plaza. The room visible behind her seemed almost bare, but clean, darned curtains hung in the windows. Seeing him rein in, she began running toward him—and she jiggled impressively, Fargo noticed.

"Mr. Fargo?" she asked again.

Fargo opened his mouth to reply, but as he got a better look at her, he was struck dumb by this sensuous vision. The Trailsman was no novice when it came to rating woman flesh, and he figured this one was at the top of the heap—far as her looks, anyway. Horn combs held her long, russet hair neatly in place, and her figure showed to curving perfection in a pinch-waisted gown of emerald green silk and lace.

"Mr. Skye Fargo?" she repeated, stopping beside the Ovaro and shading her eyes with one hand to look up at him.

In the seductive style of Santa Fe women, kohl had been artfully applied to lengthen her eyebrows, shade the lids, and extend the outer corners of the eyes. Fargo felt sudden loin warmth and was forced to discreetly shift in the saddle. He was rarely woman starved, but he often got plenty hungry.

"Excuse my bad parlor manners, miss," Fargo hastened to say, tipping his hat. "Yes, I'm Skye Fargo. May I ask how you know me?"

"Mr. Fargo, you're too modest. Any Western school child can tell you about the fearless Trailsman."

Fargo grinned, strong white teeth flashing through his beard. "School child? Well, if that includes you, maybe I'll get an education, Miss . . . ?"

"Oh, forgive me. I'm Amy Hanchon. My father, he . . ."

She faltered and Fargo waited patiently. The bell of San Antonio sounded the hour, three p.m. Wagon teams constantly brought in loads of merchant stock, and now a dozen or so wagons were parked in the plaza as the teamsters slept. Fargo spotted at least one vigilante in the shadow of the east plaza, watching him with eyes fatal as a snake.

"My father," she soldiered on bravely, knuckling away a sudden tear, "is Daniel Hanchon. Reverend Daniel Hanchon. He is . . . was also a silver miner with political aspirations. But now I'm getting ahead of myself. Mr. Fargo, would you consider working for me?"

Fargo reluctantly pried his eyes away from the creamy white swells of her bosoms, thrust high by tight stays.

"First of all, Amy, I'm curious. Even if you have heard some backcountry lore about me, how could you recognize me riding past your house? I don't pose for portraits."

"Because of the *Tucson Intelligencer*, our newspaper. You see, I tried to place a notice for the services of hired guns. The editor was sympathetic, but he was afraid to do it."

Her pretty face tightened with bitterness. "He's afraid of Henry Lutz and that despicable goon of his, Crawley Lake. Every 'man' in this region spits when Lutz says to hawk."

Fargo slanted a glance toward the vigilante in the shadows. He was looking north toward the huge church. Fargo felt a warning tingle in his scalp. Very soon he would regret not heeding it.

"Henry Lutz," he repeated. "Would that be Bearcat Lutz?"

"Yes! You know him?"

Fargo shook his head. "Know of him, is all. I hear he's the self-appointed head of the Tucson Committee for Public Safety. Anyhow, you were saying the newspaper editor was scared?"

"Yes, because I'm daring to defy Lutz. But the editor heard you were headed to Tucson to take a job with the Butterfield Overland. He said every newspaperman west of the Mississippi has heard of you."

"Yeah, I've been blessed all to hell," Fargo said from a deadpan. "But you're taking the long way around the barn, Amy. What's your dicker with Lutz?"

"He's my father's chief business rival. They are also bitter political rivals, each with a faction supporting them for Territorial Governor. Lutz is a cold-blooded murderer, but my father is the local Methodist minister, and even Lutz is afraid to openly murder a man of God. So he used his 'authority' as head of the vigilantes and arrested my father on a trumped-up charge of rape. He even paid a young Mexican girl, his own whore—I mean, mistress—to testify at the so-called miners' court."

"You're sure there's no truth to the charge?"

Red spots of anger leaped into her cheeks. "It's pure buncombe!"

"It's rough business, falling into the hands of stranglers," Fargo allowed, using the common southwest word for vigilantes. "But you need law, not me."

She placed her hands lightly on her hips. "What law? I doubt you know the half about Henry Lutz. Don't think my father is sitting in jail, Mr. Fargo. Lutz and his lick-spittles are arresting almost any man who drifts into Tucson, accusing them of peddling whiskey to the Apaches."

"That's an easy pitch right now," Fargo said. "Apaches have wiped out every white settlement except this one."

"Exactly. The prisoners spend their nights in Lutz's private prison, but from dawn until late night they work in his silver mine."

She pointed to a blue-gray line of foothills about two miles north of town. "The prison is conveniently close to the mine. So long as a man can do the donkey work, he stays alive. When he finally breaks, he's sentenced and executed. Locals are starting to call Tucson 'Hangtown.' My father is a strong man, but he's no longer young."

"I take it you want me to break him out?"

"Oh, *yes*! If he can be taken east where there's law, Lutz can't touch him. Will you do it, Mr. Fargo? Please . . . Skye?"

Fargo cursed silently. He'd rather buy ready-to-wear boots than lock horns with a criminal army. Besides, there was a contract with his name on it waiting at the Butterfield Overland office, a job that would mostly keep him away from the rattle and hullabaloo of cities.

"Lady," he finally said, "looks to me like Bearcat has the whip hand while you're trying to kick the dirt out from under your own feet. There's still soldiers at Camp Grant."

"Yes, but many are being called back east. And my father swears the commander is on Lutz's payroll."

"Even so, the plan you're backing just gives stranglers all the ammo they need to make more arrests. These hemp-committee types are gutter filth, and they *will* hang a woman—after they've had their use of her."

"That will surely happen," she warned, "if you just ride away like it's none of your business. You're the Trailsman, a supposedly brave man who takes on lost causes and wins. They say you can sniff out a rat in a pile of garbage."

"Well, 'they' make me out all wrong. I'm not the law, and I don't go sniffing for rats—I prefer to avoid them. This Lutz sounds like a hard twist, all right, but you'll need a badge toter to help you. Right now I plan to exercise my liver."

Fargo tipped his hat and took up the slack in the reins. But before he could thump the Ovaro forward, Amy laughed bitterly.

"Oh, I see. Another sawdust Casanova," she dismissed him. "It's all lies about your courage. Devilment is all you men seek."

Fargo grinned wide. "And I s'pose you're purer than Caesar's wife?"

"You've probably had her, too." Amy stamped her foot in anger. "Perverse, arrogant, and uncouth," she summed him up. A moment later, watching him, she added, "If your stupid grin grows any wider, you'll rip your cheeks."

"Tell you the straight, that acid tongue doesn't help your disposition any," Fargo retorted. "Why don't we—"

Just then the Ovaro nickered, sidestepping nervously. Fargo swallowed his sentence without finishing it, remembering the vigilante across the plaza. Fargo spotted him just as a rifle somewhere above the plaza spoke its piece, the sound whip-cracking through the lazy air.

He felt the wind-rip when a lethally close bullet snapped past his face and chewed into the baked mud of the plaza, only inches from a shocked Amy. Fargo saw her leap like a butt-shot dog, then foolishly freeze in place instead of seeking cover.

The shooter opened up in earnest, a hammering racket of gunfire. Fargo hated to do it, but rounds were peppering them nineteen-to-the-dozen, and his experienced eye told him it was Amy the shooter was after, not him—yet, fear froze her in place like a pillar of salt. So Fargo, hunched low in the saddle, planted his left boot on her chest and gave a mighty shove.

The thrust catapulted her backwards and out of immediate danger, but now the hidden shooter opened up with a vengeance on Fargo. A round whacked into his saddle, another tugged his hat off. By now, however, Fargo had followed the bullets back to their source—the bell tower of San Antonio church.

It was a job best suited for the Henry, but fractional seconds counted now, and Fargo knew his belt gun would be faster. Quicker than eyesight, he filled his hand with blue steel. Just then, up in the bell tower, he spotted the familiar glint of sunlight on skin. The Colt leaped three times in his hand. His last shot made the bell ring.

At first, when all fell silent, Fargo figured the would-be murderer had fled. Abruptly, a straw-haired man with a chiseled face and shoulders broad as a yoke appeared in the opening of the tower for a moment. Fargo thumb-cocked his Colt, ready to put sunlight through him. Before he could fire, the man suddenly plummeted to the plaza like a sack of dirt, impaling himself on the iron spikes of the church fence.

"Gone to hunt the white buffalo," Fargo muttered, leathering his six-gun. A second later a woman's shrill, piercing scream startled the yapping dogs silent.

No other series packs this much heat!

THE TRAILSMAN

**Follow the trail of the gun-slinging heroes of
Penguin's Action Westerns at
penguin.com/actionwesterns**

"A writer in the tradition of Louis L'Amour
and Zane Grey!"
—*Huntsville Times*

National Bestselling Author
RALPH COMPTON

**Available wherever books are sold or at
penguin.com**